Christmas
by Design

Cover Design by Jillian Liota, Blue Moon Creative Studio

Chapter Art from Clker-Free-Vector-Images on Pixabay

alliesambertswrites@gmail.com

www.alliesamberts.com

For anyone who needs a little magic this Christmas.

Author's Note

I WANT TO START by thanking everyone for waiting until after Thanksgiving for the release of this novella. I'm not a Scrooge, per se, but I believe Christmas season doesn't start until after Thanksgiving. Leave my turkey in peace!

But Christmas has brought me so much joy for my entire life. From bounding down the stairs to see piles of presents when I was a child to escaping into Christmas romcoms with my husband during 2020 when everything else felt so bleak, the season has always been important to me. I can probably even credit some of those romcoms with giving me the idea to start writing my own. Who knows! Magical things happen during Christmas.

More and more, as I've gotten older, Christmas has become special in so many layered ways. Memories with my family. Drinking wine in front of the fireplace. Putting together massive princess castles and intricate remote control cars after we're sure the kids have fallen asleep. Turning the Christmas tree lights to a soft white when the rest of my family is gone for a few hours. (They are fans of the rainbow lights, and they are wrong.) Reading Christmas romance books while sipping peppermint tea.

So, I thought I'd throw my hat in the ring with a Christmas novella of my own. And I am glad I did. Beckett and Gemma were so *fun* to write. The banter! The Christmas puns! The spice!

But, as with all my characters, they have backstories. Namely, Gemma experiences a lot of anxiety. She shows symptoms of that anxiety throughout the book, and she does have a panic attack on page.

If that is something that will negatively affect your mental health in any way, dear reader, you may want to put this one aside. Christmas is supposed to be filled with joy and cheer, so please take care of yourself.

And, as you may come to expect from me, my characters use profanity and are intimate. There is a multi-chapter explicit scene that spans chapters 14, 15, and 16 for you to look forward to. You probably can't avoid this one. It's substantial.

Now, get ready to snuggle up by the fire with Beckett and Gemma.

Ho Ho Ho,
Allie Santa-berts
(I'm sorry. I had to.)

Chapter 1

Beckett

GEMMA WOODARD IS A five-foot, three-inch tornado of a woman. She enters every room in a cloud of loose papers and rumpled clothes, usually with a stain or two. Her curly, auburn hair is always unruly, and her eyes are bright and fierce.

And right now, she is a giant pain in my ass.

She presses her lips together so hard they practically turn white as she violently leans back in her chair. She crosses her arms over her ample chest and stares at me across the table with those fierce eyes.

I'd be a little intimidated if I wasn't so pissed off.

Instead of retreating, I lean over the table and grit my teeth. "I don't do renovations for homeowners," I grind out, punctuating each word.

She squints at me, but her posture doesn't change. "But, why?"

"I've already told you why. I work on flipping houses without owner input *only*."

"But, *why*?" she asks again.

I muster up as much patience as I can. "That's what I like to do." I try to stay calm. "I like designing to my tastes, not a homeowner's."

She sighs heavily, which makes my blood boil. She's significantly younger than me, but she's not a teenager. I wish she wouldn't act like one.

When her gaze lands on me again, she scoffs. "That is a stupid reason not to take on this project." She starts gesturing so wildly, I'm afraid she's going to knock over the coffee cup sitting near her right elbow. "It's a historic house. We'd be preserving actual local history. Restoring it to its former glory."

"Northwest Indiana is not local," I say tersely.

She throws her hands up in the air and knocks the coffee cup in the process. By some miracle, it teeters but doesn't tip over. "Do you ever get out of your Chicago bubble, or are you too busy being grumpy in your penthouse apartment to go slumming it in Indiana for a few days a week?" She makes an over-exaggerated pout and raises her eyebrows to taunt me.

She's trying to rile me up. I know she is. She's well aware that I don't live in a penthouse apartment. I live in a top-floor condo on Clark Street with a gorgeous view of the Chicago skyline. It's a very nice apartment, but it's not a penthouse. She wants to make me self-conscious of my wealth, which she does every time we disagree. We don't work together often, but each time in the past year since she was hired as a project manager has been like this.

It's not my fault I worked my way up to a high-paying, corporate interior design gig before leaving that world to start flipping houses.

No matter. She can't rile me up because I don't care. I'm not taking this project. I'm especially not working with this messy, chronically tardy, tornado of a woman.

Our boss and the owner of the house-flipping firm we both work for, Jacob Drawley, pinches the bridge of his nose and takes a deep breath. "Let's not go there, please. I don't need another run-in with HR."

Jacob and I went to design school together. We both got into high-paying, stable design jobs, but he was never happy with that move. This company was sort of a midlife crisis project for him. When he started it four years ago, he called me out of the blue and asked if I might want to join him. At thirty-six and also disillusioned with the business world, I took on one flip and fell in love. I started part time while keeping my other job as a safety net. In the past four years, he's grown this company—Designs by Drawley—into a thriving, profitable business. So profitable, actually, that he offered me a decent salary to come work for him full time. A year ago, I did just that.

Gemma harumphs and crosses her arms again. I take great joy in her being chastised, and I smirk. From the way she flares her nostrils at me, she doesn't like my expression one bit.

"I'll ask you this, then," she addresses Jacob. He tenses ever so slightly. I can't blame him; she's scary when she's angry. "Are you requesting we work on this project together, or are you telling us we have to?" She looks back at me with an expression that reads, *checkmate*.

I keep my own countenance completely neutral as I turn my attention to Jacob. He offered to make me part-owner last year, shortly before he hired Gemma, but I declined. I left my last job to focus more on design. I didn't want to leap right back into a more managerial role. So, *technically*, he could demand I take on this project, but he wouldn't.

Would he?

He catches my eye and winces in apology.

Fuck.

"I don't want to *make* you do it," he says to me. "But I want the company to take this on. So far, we've been doing only flips of cheap, run-down houses without owners. A home renovation would be new for us. It could open up a larger clientele."

I tip my chin in Gemma's direction. "Let her do it and pull a junior designer off another project," I suggest, but even as I do, I know it's not possible. All the junior designers are already stretched thin, and Jacob is a big, soft, family guy. With Christmas coming up, everyone is looking to take time off. And he's asking me now because that's not an issue for me. I live alone, and I like it that way.

I eye Gemma across the table. She's got a kid at home, so it makes no sense to me why she'd be jumping to manage a new project this close to Christmas, or why Jacob would even ask her, considering his devotion to family time.

"You know we can't do that right before the holidays," he confirms my suspicions. "And, besides, being our first historical home renovation, I want my two best people on it."

Gemma practically preens at the compliment, but I know he's just trying to butter me up so I'll agree to take this on. She shoots me a sidelong glance and deflates a bit when she sees I'm not going to give in so easily.

"Oh, come on, Scrooge," she jabs. "We'll look at the blueprints, put together some samples and call some contractors, drive out to Indiana, take a look at the house, write up a proposal, and go on our merry way just in time for Christmas. We can finish the job after the holidays." She pauses to consider, then says, "Well, *I* will be going on my merry way. *You'll* probably just go home and grump around."

I gesture toward her as I address Jacob, "You expect me to work with her when she says things like that?"

Jacob gives her a warning glare, and she throws her hands up in surrender. "My bad. I'm sure Beks has a perfectly lovely Christmas planned where he'll be surrounded by family and friends singing carols by the fire and sipping hot chocolate." She looks straight at me and says, "Sorry."

She doesn't sound at all sorry.

I throw a hand in her direction again and look at Jacob, who jumps in before I can say anything. "I'm starting to think pairing you two together again isn't a great idea. I really thought two people with your level of combined experience would be a dream team. But I can see now that it won't work." He sighs as he runs a hand over his unshaved jaw. He looks more haggard than usual, which is saying a lot. He's not the type to get a full eight hours of sleep each night. "I guess we'll just have to pass on this one. Or see if Mrs. Dash can extend her project deadline so we can start after the holidays."

Jacob's shoulders slump forward. He frowns at his desk calendar, flipping through January, February, and into March. Gemma looks more and more dejected with each flip of the page. She must have really wanted this project. God knows why. She's a mess of a person, but she's extremely talented. She can certainly do better than a home renovation.

"If you're not taking this on, Beckett, you can leave," Jacob says without looking up. "We'll see you Monday."

I nod once, push my chair away, and stand. But in that motion, I inadvertently lock eyes with Gemma. Her rusty eyebrows tip up and pinch together a bit. Her deep, green eyes are big and round. They'd be almost pretty if they hadn't been locked on me with hatred just a moment ago. She flicks her gaze to Jacob, who is still poring over his calendar, then back to me. When I don't say anything, she sags—actually *sags*—and starts chewing on the corner of her mouth as she stares at the table in front of her.

Why does she want this so badly? What's in it for her if she takes it? She's had her pick of projects since she started here, I thought. Though, I'm not as well-versed in the behind-the-scenes of the company as an actual partner would be. Something isn't adding up.

But she looks so impossibly sad about the prospect of losing this house renovation. I glance behind Jacob to the windows that show only the dreary, Chicago winter. It hasn't snowed yet, but the gray sky seems to indicate it will soon. Across the street, I can see a man in a bright red Santa hat ringing a bell next to a charity bucket. Colorful lights are starting to blink on as the sun sets earlier each day.

For a second, a glimmer of Christmas generosity sparks in my chest. Gemma was right about this being a quick project. A day or so in Indiana looking at a house, and an easy proposal. Some phone calls from the office to organize everything, and another trip or two out there to make sure it's done right. It'd be no sweat, really. It wouldn't be done before Christmas, but some of the checks would clear, which would help out the firm. And if Jacob thinks it would be good for us to branch out, maybe I can find some Christmas spirit and take one for the team.

But she was right about another thing, too. I do spend my Christmases alone. She was wrong about me being a grump about it, though. I prefer a silent night with my roaring fireplace, a glass of brandy, a book, and my cat. It's a nice reset before the end of the year. Most importantly, it's quiet.

I look forward to it every year.

I watch Gemma for a second as she leans forward on her elbows, trying to affect an air of calm. A tick in her jaw and the way she digs the pads of her fingers into her forearms give her away, though. Her nails are bitten to the quick, and the skin on her hands is dry. There's paint smudged near her elbow, and another stain of something unidentifiable on her torn jeans. Her reddish hair is pulled into a mass of curls on top of her head, as if she couldn't care less what she looks like.

This is how this woman shows up to work. Unbelievable.

No, I can't work with her on this. It's a new venture for the company, which makes it completely unpredictable. Add Gemma the Tornado to the mix, and it could be a disaster. I'll enjoy my clean, quiet Christmas and come back to work on some more stable projects.

If she wants to spend her holiday season going back and forth to Northwest Indiana, let her. I do not.

Chapter 2

Gemma

It's Saturday in mid-December, and State Street is absolutely packed with tourists. I'm a born-and-raised suburbanite—and I still live in the suburbs with my daughter and, since her father left us high and dry, my parents—but Chicago has always had this pull on me. It's a major reason why I applied for the project manager job at Designs by Drawley, even though I knew it would mean a lot of commuting and more time away from my daughter, Nova. I can't afford to live within Chicago city limits, so any time in the city is better than no time in the city.

That's what I mumble to myself, anyway, as I grip Nova's tiny hand tighter. There are veritable throngs of people moving slowly past the giant holiday window displays at Macy's, and Nova, of course, insists on walking by herself rather than being carried. And she's only two, so she's even slower than the tourists.

"Oh, look at the pretty snowflakes!" I say to her while pointing at the glittery crystals lining one of the windows. A snowman moves back and forth as fake snow falls behind it.

"Up, Mama! I see," Nova whines. I grab her under her armpits and swing her around to balance her on my hip. I grunt as she twists and leans forward as if she wants to leap out of my arms. My grasp on her tightens.

"Isn't it pretty?" I ask.

She nods enthusiastically. "Snow!" She laughs and tilts her head up to the dreary, darkening sky. A cold drizzle had started to fall about half an hour ago.

"No, baby, that's rain," I correct her. She wrinkles her little nose, and I chuckle. "Yeah, I don't like it either. That's Chicago weather for you."

"Chi-ca-go." She tries out the syllables slowly, wrapping her mouth around each one. Her wide eyes turn away from me and toward the brightly colored windows. "Pretty."

It is pretty. The whole city is lit up and alive with holiday spirit. I look up at the glittering trumpets lining the building, but a drop of water lands right in my eye. I wipe it away and try not to grumble. The whole point of this outing was for Nova to experience some of Chicago's Christmas joy, and so joyful I shall remain.

I glance in front of us. Two more windows before the end, and I think she's tired because she wraps her little arms around my neck and buries her face in my shoulder. The pom-pom on her hat tickles my cheek.

"Okay, Star-baby," I say softly. "Let's see the last couple of windows and get some hot chocolate. Sound good?"

She nods without lifting her head from my shoulder, but she turns her face outward so she can see. We walk slowly—but faster now that I'm carrying her—to take a look at the last two displays, then I swing us around the corner and into the store. There's a coffee shop on the first level that, with any luck, won't have much of a line.

I turn toward the shop and stop in my tracks. The line is at least twenty people deep.

When did Christmas get so *crowded*?

Nova feels heavier in my arms all of a sudden, and I look down to see her eyes drooping closed. I'll never say it out loud, but my mom was right when she said Nova is too young for this to be fun. I didn't care. I just wanted to share some holiday cheer with my daughter. Is that too much to ask for?

Apparently, it is.

I glance toward the door, where the rain is really coming down now. I look back at the line, which seems to be moving at a decent pace. There are four baristas behind that tiny counter.

Hot chocolate or dragging a sleepy Nova all the way back to my car in the rain. That's not even a choice. I slide into the back of the line and shift Nova higher on my hip. She barely even stirs.

About thirty minutes later, I'm finally at the counter. Nova has perked up with the proximity to hot chocolate. So have I, honestly. She's getting wriggly, so I set her down before ordering for us. Two hot chocolates with extra whipped cream and a cake pop for good measure. Nova reaches to grab the counter ledge so she can get up on her tiptoes to see over it. I hand over my card and gently squeeze the little pom-pom on top of her hat. She smiles up at me like I'm the most important person in her world. My heart—already overflowing with love for her, for the season, for this city—grows even more.

"Um, I'm sorry, ma'am." The barista says, and I tear my attention away from my kid. "Your card has been declined?"

"What?" I frown. I'm sure I had enough money for this excursion on this card. I'm positive, actually. Things have been tight, especially as I've been trying to save for a house of our own, but I planned this trip down to the penny. Unless...

I glance at the clock on the card reader. Five o'clock on the dot. My parking meter must have run out. The parking app I use would have automatically charged me for another hour. I hadn't calculated getting hot chocolate to take this long.

I curse under my breath and toss my diaper bag on the counter so I can rifle through it. I never carry cash, but I also never clean this thing out, so there's a possibility I could get lucky today. It is the holiday season, after all. Isn't there supposed to be some guardian angel looking out for me or something? Some kind of Christmas miracle waiting to happen?

Nova, sensing something is wrong, hugs my leg and starts to whimper.

"I know, baby." I try to keep my voice soothing, but my breathing is starting to get shallow. It feels like something is squeezing my chest. "Just give me a second. I'm sure I have something in here." My heart starts beating faster, and my breath is coming in shorter gasps. It's the type of anxiety I probably won't recover from for the entire evening, but I try to keep it cool for her sake.

I can sense the people behind me getting frustrated, which makes me even more agitated. The last thing I want to do is tell Nova we can't have this little treat. It's under fifteen dollars. What kind of parent am I if I can't even treat my kid to something that costs less than fifteen dollars?

And that's the thought that has tears pricking at the corners of my eyes. *I will not cry in the Macy's café in front of Nova and all these people*, I tell myself, though it does little to lessen the anxiety. If anything, it makes it heavier. Nova squeezes my leg tighter.

God, I am the absolute worst parent in the world right now. I'm sure of it.

A big hand touches my elbow. I jump at the contact, which causes a couple of the tears I had been barely holding at bay to trickle down my cheeks. I hastily wipe them away and put an arm around Nova.

"Allow me." A voice so silken it sounds absolutely decadent comes from my left. It's soft and reassuring. A guardian angel, indeed. That voice alone manages to take my anxiety down just enough for me to turn and look at the man who is handing his card over to the barista.

My arm around Nova stiffens as I take in the extremely handsome man who smells deliciously like rosemary. I scan my way up, past his navy wool peacoat, clean-shaven jaw, and land on the excellently coiffed salt-and-pepper hair of Beckett Camdon.

Oh, hell no. This is the man that cost me the historical house project that I desperately wanted to take on, because how fucking cool would it be to work on a historical house? Not only that, the bonus that Jacob pays for each project would also be the difference between me putting a down payment on a home of my own and living with my parents for the next six months. Sure, the bonus wouldn't clear until the new year, but without Beckett, now I have to wait for one of the junior designers to be free. And they are wretched. Sexist assholes, every one of them. Beckett hates me, but at least it's not because I'm a woman.

But no. This man had to stand between me and my Christmas spirit.

He's no guardian angel. And I certainly don't care if he's hot as hell in that peacoat. He's the Scroogiest of Scrooges, and there is no way I'm letting him buy our hot chocolates.

Except I've been frozen in shock, and the barista is already handing his card back to him. When I don't move to grab the drinks she's holding out for me, Beckett takes the smallest and bends down to hand it to Nova. She squeals with joy.

The barista clears her throat, and the woman behind me sighs deeply.

"Yeah, yeah," I grumble. I take my hot chocolate and the paper bag with Nova's cake pop before moving out of the way.

"Sank you," Nova lisps, cupping her mittened hands around the hot chocolate.

"No problem," Beckett says, his voice impossibly kind and warm. His eyes crinkle at the corners briefly as he looks at her with clear affection.

I don't know who this man is, but he's not the Beckett Camdon who coldly denied working with me yesterday afternoon in Jacob's office.

He straightens, his ice-blue eyes meeting mine. They're frigid again, as if I don't deserve the warmth he was just directing toward my daughter. Could he be any more obvious? I'm sure it wasn't the project he was rejecting, but working with me. I'm not surprised. All the men at the office are like this—and Designs by Drawley is made up of mostly men. They don't want to work with a thirty-year-old single mom who rushes out the door every morning with unruly hair I don't have time to do and fresh toddler stains on her clothes. It doesn't matter that I'm a damn good project manager. They see me and run for the hills. Or, worse, say a bunch of sexist shit I have to pretend to ignore.

Which is also why I needed this project to fill out the down payment on a house. I have trouble finding people to work with. And Beckett said no.

Typical.

His gaze lingers on me for a moment longer before he nods curtly. "Woodard," he says as if my name tastes bad in his mouth.

"Imagine seeing you here, Becky." I use one of my endless supply of nicknames for him because it pisses him off. I'm rewarded for my efforts with his narrowed eyes.

"Becky!" Nova shouts, and I bark out a laugh. It's probably the lingering adrenaline from my near-panic attack that makes me laugh so loudly, but it feels good. Beckett's face is impassive, though I think I see a corner of his mouth tick up as he looks down at her again. It's gone too fast to be sure.

His gaze slides back up to me. I'm not really sure why he's still standing here, empty-handed and just looking at me.

It finally occurs to me that he didn't order anything back there. I raise an eyebrow at him. "What, no coffee as black as your heart to stoke the devil-fire in your belly?" I ask.

That corner of his mouth ticks again, but this time it looks more like a twitch than a glimmer of amusement. He glances at Nova, then back to me. "At least one of you has some manners," he drawls. "And no, I wasn't in line for coffee. I'm here to find a gift for my mother."

I tilt my head and hum. "So, he *does* have family," I muse. "I don't suppose *she* taught you *your* excellent manners?"

He purses his lips as he regards me with that icy stare. "She taught me enough that I wouldn't let a woman hold up the line for coffee."

I shrug a shoulder. I'm suddenly too tired for a witty comeback. Anxiety will do that to you. But I'm also not thanking this asshole. Fifteen dollars is nothing for a guy who lives in a penthouse apartment. *Okay*, not a penthouse, but I know it's still expensive, and I'm sure it's pretty sweet. It's the least he can do after costing me my own house.

"See you Monday, Beckster." I take Nova's hand and try to pull her past him, since he's dead set on just standing there.

But Nova removes her hand out from mine so she can wave enthusiastically at Beckett. "Bye-bye, Becky! Merry Christmas!" She beams at him.

I could swear he softens just a fraction. He actually waves back, which would be sweet in any other circumstance.

But I cackle coldly. "Yeah, Becky. Merry Christmas."

Chapter 3

Beckett

DESPITE WHAT GEMMA WOODARD might think of me, I'm not a heartless bastard. My mother did, in fact, teach me how to treat women right. She raised me by herself; my dad left before I can even remember. She had a boyfriend when I was around seven years old, and he left, too. Broke both our damn hearts. After that, it was just me and her, forever.

When I saw Gemma on Saturday as I entered Macy's, her movements were choppy and laced with panic. Her little girl was squeezing her leg as if she, too, were afraid of something. Or, maybe, like she felt she could single-handedly keep her mom from crumpling into an anxious puddle on the floor. I remember moments like that from my own childhood—my mom crying over bills when she thought I was in bed, or her telling me I couldn't have a toy from the dollar aisle because we couldn't afford it.

So, there was only one thing to do. Pay for her order.

Who says I have no Christmas spirit?

Well, Gemma seems to think so. I'm not sure why she hates me so much, but she clearly does.

It isn't until Sunday afternoon that I realize she must have needed that historical house renovation to make ends meet. She's not paid the same salary I am. Jacob pays most of his employees smaller salaries, and then they receive bonuses for each house that sells. Gemma must see this one as a sure thing since the old woman who owns the house isn't moving, so the owner will pay for the renovations no matter what.

I prevented Gemma from getting the money from the start of this project. So, just like Saturday, I do the only thing there is to do. I call Jacob and tell him I've changed my mind.

See? I'm brimming with Christmas spirit. Which is why I'm shocked when, almost immediately upon entering my office on Monday morning, the door opens and slams shut before I have even dropped my bag on the floor next to my desk.

I turn around slowly. Gemma is standing there, breathing heavily. Her cheeks are flushed prettily, and her green eyes are on fire in a way that stirs something deep inside me.

But I try to ignore whatever that is, because she's definitely not here to thank me.

She doesn't seem to be here to say anything at all, just breathe loudly and stare at me as if she could shoot lasers out of her eyeballs. I take my time removing my coat and hanging it up. By the time I lower myself into my chair and look back at her, her face is even redder, her eyes are even more fiery, and I still have no fucking clue what's going on.

"Can I help you, Woodard?" I ask, keeping my tone measured. The last thing I need is for her to fly off the handle.

"I don't need your pity," she snaps.

I huff. "What would possibly give you the impression that I pity you?"

She clenches and unclenches her fists at her sides. "You saw me looking for cash, assumed I needed some kind of knight in shining armor, and paid for my order. And then, you took a project you don't want because you feel bad for me."

"I wasn't—" I start, but she cuts me off by slamming some cash on my desk.

"I didn't need you to pay for my hot chocolate," she says between clenched teeth.

"Okay..." I say slowly, sparing a glance for the crumpled bills on my desk.

But she's not done. "I can take care of myself," she insists, tilting her chin up and folding her arms.

"I have no doubt—"

"And I can take care of my child." That's when her voice cracks slightly. Just enough to be noticeable. She clenches her jaw against it, as if steeling herself could erase the sound.

I don't pity her. I wasn't lying about that. But the way she falters opens something inside me I have a feeling will be difficult to close.

Standing slowly, I remove my wallet from my back pocket. I wasn't going to take her money, but it's clear to me that this is about more than a couple bucks. I take my time fitting the bills into my wallet, then lay it on the desk before meeting her gaze again.

"As I was saying, I have no doubt you can care for yourself and your daughter." I ensure my voice stays quiet and neutral. "I thought I was doing a nice thing. Spreading some Christmas cheer, if you will. I can see now that you didn't need any extra cheer. I apologize. It won't happen again."

Her shoulders relax slightly, though her arms stay folded. "Good."

"And as for the Indiana house, I simply changed my mind."

Her shoulders and jaw tense again. "You 'changed your mind'"—she practically air-quotes the words—"because you thought I needed this gig after your misguided chivalry on Saturday."

I shake my head. "I thought about what you said. Preserving local history is important, and I know the company could benefit from diversifying our offerings."

She eyes me skeptically as she raises an eyebrow. "Really." It's meant to be a question, but it doesn't sound like one.

I run my hand through my hair. "Look. This isn't public knowledge, but profit margins aren't what they once were. Real estate prices are increasing. Homebuyers are more and more skeptical of flips after seeing disasters and lawsuits over houses from those television shows. If I'm doing this for anyone, I'm doing it for Jacob." I sit back down and rifle idly through some papers on my desk, hoping she can't see through the half-lie.

She narrows her eyes. "You aren't doing this in part because of Saturday?"

I sigh out a quick puff of air. She's not going to let this go unless I really drive it home. "Woodard, what about me suggests I would take on a project with a homeowner who surely has opinions about her house, in Indiana, three weeks before Christmas—with *you* of all people—out of some 'misguided chivalry?'"

I lock eyes with her, and we stare at each other for long enough that it starts getting uncomfortable. But if she won't back down, neither will I. She needs this project whether she wants to admit it to me or not.

Eventually, she presses her lips into a tight line and nods curtly. She turns on her heel and pulls open my office door.

I blow out a long breath through pursed lips. "Can't wait to work with you, Woodard," I mumble under my breath, my voice dripping with sarcasm. I really hope I didn't make a mistake agreeing to this project.

"I heard that, Bucky," she calls back just as the door closes behind her.

She levels a glare at me through the window next to the door. Her eyes track me as she walks slowly out of sight. When she can't twist her head around to glare at me any longer, she turns to walk backwards. She keeps me in her line of sight until her entire body disappears from my view.

It's so ridiculous that I can't help but chuckle. Fortunately, I'm able to hold in my laughter until she's out of earshot. The last thing I need is for her to know I find her antics amusing. It'll only encourage her.

Chapter 4

Gemma

"No, no, no, no, no," I groan as my car shudders. I smack the steering wheel, but a loud whine comes from somewhere in front of me. "Oh, baby, I'm so sorry," I purr. It can't hurt to change my tactics, right? I pet the dashboard gently for good measure, but it's no use. The car sputters as I throw on my flashers and pull carefully over to the shoulder. Someone honks angrily at me as they speed by. I wave my middle finger out the driver's side window as I pull on my emergency break, but he's long gone.

And I'm stuck here. On I-80. I didn't even make it out of Illinois.

To top it off, I'm exhausted. Nova was awake three times last night. She wasn't upset or anything, just babbling, but since we share a room, I was awake, too.

Today is the day Beckett and I are supposed to have our initial meeting with Mrs. Emelia Dash, the owner of the historical house in Indiana we're renovating. We were going to tour the place and get some ideas from her about what she wants for her home. I was going to start the project that was going to finally give me enough money for a down payment on a house.

Now, if I can even make it there, I'll have to spend the money on a new car. If I didn't have my kid to cart around, I could take the train into the city every day for work and hold off. Alas, for me, a car is a necessity.

And the worst part about all of this is that Beckett Camdon, Certified Loner Himself, had offered to give me a ride. "Don't read into it, Woodard," he had said gruffly after I teased him for being nice. "You're literally on the way."

But I had insisted, yet again, that I didn't need his handouts. I would drive myself, thank-you-very-much. I'm not an idiot. I know what he's doing. "Spreading some Christmas cheer," my ass. That man has about as much Christmas cheer in his entire body as I have in my left pinky. He says buying my hot chocolate wasn't pity, but I know better. And now, he can't stop himself.

But my fifteen-year-old, two-hundred-thousand-mile Honda has other ideas, apparently. She's had a good life, this car. She's treated me well.

I try to get the engine to turn over again, hopeful that after a minute of rest, she'll come back to life.

No such luck. She's dead.

I stare out over the dashboard for another minute as I bite my fingernails. I could call roadside assistance and have them tow the car. I'm not that far from home, so I could also call my dad to pick me up. He's the most wonderful man in the entire world. He'd drive me to Indiana and back without even batting an eye. But a quick glance at the clock tells me I'm already dangerously close to being late. If I have to wait for my dad to come get me, I'll be rolling in about an hour after I promised to be there. And I can already hear Beckett's exasperated sigh and see his chiseled features tighten in annoyance.

Nothing left to do but swallow my pride.

I open my phone and tap Beckett's number before I can think better of it.

I keep chewing my nails as it rings once, twice, three times.

"Woodard," his growly voice comes over the line. "Let me guess. You're late."

"Good morning to you, too, Beckie-Bear." I cringe silently at that nickname. I started taunting him shortly after I was hired, mostly because he refused to use my first name, so I refused to use his. That, and it was so easy to get under his skin. He's always so proper and put-together. I figured someone could take him down a peg. Now, it would feel weird if I stopped, but that one wasn't my best work.

He's silent for a long moment, and I can hear the sounds of his fancy car flying over the highway. "You needed something?" he asks flatly.

"Um..." I trail off. This is going to hurt, but I'm starting to be able to see my breath now that the heat isn't running. "Where are you, and do you think you could stop and help a damsel in distress on the shoulder of eastbound I-80?" I try to keep my tone light, but I drop my forehead to the steering wheel as I squeeze my eyes shut. That did hurt. A lot.

He's silent again, and this time I can cut the tension coming over the line with a knife. He's not happy about this. I can tell by his heavy breathing.

"What mile marker?" His voice is terse. I wince at the sound of it.

I squint into the rising winter sun. "I can see the exit for Dixie Highway. I think I'm just west of Homewood?"

"It's your lucky day, Woodard. I'm about ten minutes behind you." Thankfully, his voice has lost its tightness. It's not friendly. I'm not sure he's capable of that. But it's not irritated.

I breathe out a sigh of relief. "Great. Awesome. Thank you so much."

"Don't mention it," he says and hangs up immediately.

I tilt my head all the way back to bang against the headrest, clutching my phone in my un-gloved hand. Driving to Indiana and back with Beckett Camdon is not how I wanted the day to go, but things could be worse. At least he was on his way, and I'm not stranded.

I give myself an extra minute to take a few deep breaths, then dial my dad's number. He answers on the first ring.

"Hey Gemmy-bear. Nova is here eating oatmeal. She loves it! Don't you, Star-baby?"

I can't help but smile, even despite being broken down on the side of the highway. My dad loves his granddaughter beyond reason. He and my mom are not only my current landlords, but they're also my daycare. I know how fortunate I am to have them in my corner. Lots of people don't have the support of their families, and I have it in spades. But it doesn't make it any easier to ask them for help.

"That's great, Dad. What flavor is it?" I'm stalling in this sweet moment for as long as I can.

"Strawberries and cream. That was always your favorite, too." I can hear the smile in his voice.

"Still is. Listen..." I trail off and bring my nails to my mouth again. They'll be nonexistent by the end of this project if things keep going this way. "My car broke down on the highway. It's okay!" I add quickly, before he can get too concerned. "I'm okay. I'll get it towed. My coworker is a little behind me, so he's going to pick me up. But the car will probably sit here for a while, and I didn't want you to worry."

"Do you want me to come out there and deal with the tow truck, Bear? I don't mind. Your mom can stay here with Nova."

I close my eyes and let out a tight breath. "No, that's okay. I'll... deal with it."

"I can at least get it to a garage for you," he offers again.

I bark out a tight laugh. "It probably belongs in the scrapyard."

"Well, yeah," he admits with a much lighter chuckle than mine. He's never liked me driving this old car on the highway to and from work. "You sure you're okay, Gemmy? You sound stressed."

That's an understatement. Planning Christmas for a toddler, trying to buy my own place, working with Mr. Grump on a project he never wanted in the first place, not being able to afford hot chocolate, and now car trouble on top of it. Stressed doesn't begin to cover it.

I put on my happiest face, even though he can't see me. Fake it till you make it, I guess. "I'm fine, Daddy," I say cheerfully. "It was just unexpected, that's all."

"Okay, sweetie. Well, let us know when you've gotten there safe. We miss you, don't we?" That last question was addressed to Nova, who coos sweetly in the background.

We say our goodbyes, and I start to rummage around in the glovebox for the number for roadside assistance. I'm so focused on trying to find it that I jump about a foot when someone taps at my passenger side door. My hand flies to my chest, and my breath starts coming rapidly.

"Shit. You scared me!" I shout at Beckett's scowling face as he leans over to look in the window. He pulls the door open and crunches his long legs into the passenger seat, adjusting his wool coat as he sits. He closes the door quickly, then twists to look at me.

His scowl deepens as he looks me up and down. Probably assessing the stains on my clothes or something.

"Are you okay?" he asks harshly.

"Wow. Try not to care too much," I fire back. I am in a mood now, and he's just stoking the fire with his shitty attitude.

He swallows as his bushy black eyebrows knit together. "You're okay," he says again. This time, it's not a question.

"I'm fine. It's my car that's broken," I remind him.

He looks me up and down again. Was he... worried? No. There's no way.

But he doesn't say anything, and him wordlessly staring at me is starting to get weird. I decide to break the silence since he's not going to do it. "I was just going to call a tow—"

"I did already," he interrupts me.

I blink a few times. The cold is starting to addle my brain, I think. "You what?"

"I called a tow truck. They should be here in half an hour. We can wait with the car if you want. Or they said they could tow it to the nearest garage for us to pick up on the way back."

I tick an eyebrow up. "Did you think my lady brain couldn't process what to do about my little car trouble?"

He rears back a bit in his seat. "No. Why would I think that?"

I press my lips together, then take a deep breath. "You must not have been on a job site with a woman in a while. Insulting my gender is kind of par for the course."

Beckett goes back to regarding me silently, though this time he looks a little curious. It's unnatural, seeing so many emotions on his face in one interaction. I'd kind of like it if it weren't so off-putting. After a minute, he shakes his head as if to clear it. "I know a guy out this way. He works on my car. I called him because I didn't know if you had roadside assistance."

"You bring your car all the way out to Homewood to get an oil change?" I ask skeptically. "There's no one nearer to your penthouse?"

"I don't have a penthouse, and he's the best." He shrugs a shoulder as if it's nothing.

"Of course he is." I roll my head against the headrest so I can see out the windshield. I sigh, defeated. "He's probably expensive, too."

"He owes me one," Beckett says.

I whip my head to him. "No."

"No, what?"

"Just no. You're not paying to tow my car."

He looks at me as if I must be even more stupid than he originally thought. "You're right. I'm not. He owes me," he repeats slowly, as if he's talking to an idiot.

"Then use the favor on yourself."

He scoffs. "My car isn't going to break down."

"How could I forget?" I ask sardonically. "Only the best for Beckett Camdon."

I could swear his light blue eyes flash at the use of his full name. Probably out of anger. Or surprise. He clears his throat. "Do you want to wait with your car?" The question is gentle and laced with understanding. Not sympathy, though. He's just being... nice. Which is unexpectedly attractive. But it's also clear he's not letting me call my own tow truck. Which might actually also be him being nice.

It completely throws me off.

"Uh..." I stammer. I run a hand over the steering wheel, willing the lump in my throat not to rise. This car has been with me through a lot. Saying goodbye to her on the side of the road is making me gloomy.

Beckett, to his credit, just waits for me. It doesn't feel impatient or moody. It almost feels like he understands.

"No," I say finally. "This has been a long time coming. I kind of doubt your guy will even think it's worth fixing. Let's just go." I slide my gaze from the dashboard to meet his, which is impassively trained on me. "But it's your lucky day. You get to spend *even more* time with me." I forcefully twist my mouth into a cheesy grin.

"Oh, joy," he responds with zero emotion.

There's the Beckett I know. It settles me to be on firmer ground with him. I tap the steering wheel once and check my rearview mirror before stepping out of the car. He follows behind.

Chapter 5

Beckett

FOR AN ENTIRE WEEK, I couldn't get the image of Gemma searching for money in her bag out of my mind. She said I pity her. I don't. She might be a bit of a mess, but she's a strong woman. I've heard her talking to contractors on the phone at the office. She doesn't take any shit from anyone. But seeing her near panic brought up some memories of my mom that I thought I had hidden long ago.

Any time I've tried to talk to her about the project in the past few days, she closes off. It's like her perpetual brightness has been replaced by skepticism. I've found that I don't like it very much.

So, when she called me on my way to the Dash house and her voice sounded shaky and defeated, something came over me. As if watching her cynicism grow by the day has changed me in some way, and listening to her breaking up is just too much to bear.

I don't hesitate. I step on the gas and call my car guy on the way to her.

I can't name the feeling I get when I slide into the passenger seat of her car and see she's okay. She hadn't told me what happened. For all I knew, her car was on fire. So when I see her, I can't help but check her over. The worst I can say for her is that her nails are bitten to all hell, and her nose is pink with cold.

She's just... fine.

But that's probably the best I can say for her, too, as she sits in my car saying nothing, alternating between chewing on her lip and her nails, watching the bland, winter scenery pass us by for the entirety of the drive to the Dash house.

If she wants to drive in silence, that's fine by me. I prefer it. But I can't shake the feeling that I should say *something*, if only to stop her from chewing on her thoughts along with her fingernails.

I wish I were better at small talk. Forty years old, and I've never been able to master the skill. If anything, it's gotten worse as I've gotten older. Probably because I see less and less of a need to make other people comfortable the longer I'm on this planet. But it doesn't change the fact that, right now, it would be a nice skill to have.

When we pull up to the Dash house, though, Gemma gasps. Honestly, I share the sentiment. The house is, in a word, enormous. It's two full stories tall with dormer windows on a smaller, third floor—probably an attic. There's a huge wrap-around porch and multiple entrances. From where we sit, it appears as if the siding and porch have been refinished. It looks brand new. The siding is painted a bright canary yellow, and the porch and surrounding fence have been whitewashed. Not my first choice of color scheme, but I remind myself that this design project isn't about what I'd pick. I'm begrudgingly here to make Mrs. Dash happy.

Upon further inspection, the windows look warped. The sunlight reflected in the panes is distorted, and there's a classic diamond pattern in some of them. Leaded glass, most likely. Interesting.

I take in the landscape as well. This huge, old farmhouse stands on one hundred acres of land in Northwest Indiana. It would be the perfect location for a bed and breakfast or a wedding venue, both possibilities I know Gemma has talked to Mrs. Dash about.

The front door opens, and exactly the type of old woman I'd expect to own this place walks out. Her hair is gray and pulled into a loose bun on the top of her head. She's wearing an old, brown crew neck sweatshirt and baggy jeans that are hastily shoved into boots as if she pulled them on when she saw us approach. She tugs a huge, crocheted shawl over her shoulders against the chill of the December morning. She looks like she could be a farmer's wife, though I know this land hasn't been used for any real farming for at least a decade.

Gemma wastes no time getting out of the car. She doesn't even spare me a glance as she pushes her door open and steps out. It makes me wonder if the drive was so unbearable that she can't stand to be in this car with me for one minute longer. The thought of it sends an unexpected pang through my chest. *What the fuck?* I rub at it as if that could take the feeling away.

"Good morning, Mrs. Dash!" she calls as she slams the door shut behind her. I still need a minute to recover from that strange feeling, but it looks like I don't have one. I scramble to turn the car off and get out, feeling uneven and a bit shaky.

Mrs. Dash meets Gemma about halfway to the porch, and I'm bringing up the rear just as a huge, gray dog comes bounding out the front door. No, that's not a dog. That's more like a *horse*. I freeze, and I must make a noise because Gemma whips around to see me standing there, wide-eyed, staring at this monster creature who seems to only have eyes for me.

Gemma doesn't hesitate. She steps right in front of the dog, drops to her knees, and opens her arms wide. That *thing* bounds right into her open arms. She wraps it in a hug of sorts as she rubs its ears and lets it lick her face.

Disgusting.

"And who is this magnificent beast?" she croons, looking up at Mrs. Dash while the thing continues to press its flat tongue against her cheek and neck.

"This is Periwinkle. We call him Perry for short."

"Periwinkle?" I choke out, my voice higher than I expected it to be. I clear my throat.

Mrs. Dash laughs. It's a deep, breathy sound. "My son named him a long time ago." She eyes me carefully. "He's big, but he's old and practically blind. He won't hurt you."

"Sure," I mumble under my breath.

Gemma must hear me, though, because she huffs. "Not a fan of dogs?"

I take a moment to straighten my wool coat and brush some lint off the front. "No," I say with finality.

"The feeling is probably mutual," she mutters only loud enough for me to hear as she scratches under the dog's chin. "Dogs are excellent judges of character."

"Perry, go chase something," Mrs. Dash commands with a clap. The dog regards her for a moment, then bounds off into the distance. "Don't worry about him. He won't be back for hours. He's an outside dog, that one." She crosses the distance between us and extends a hand to me as Gemma stands and brushes herself off. "Emelia Dash. Such a pleasure to meet you both."

I shake her hand firmly. "Beckett Camdon, interior designer," I introduce myself. "We've spoken on the phone."

She nods and extends her hand to Gemma, who takes it and shakes enthusiastically.

"Gemma Woodard. I'll be the project manager for your renovation." She looks up at the house and a smile lights up her entire face. "I have to say, I'm really excited for this."

Mrs. Dash grins as she turns and walks briskly toward the house. "Well, come on in out of the cold. I imagine you want to see what you're working with."

Confidence regained, I lean in slightly as I pass Gemma on my way into the house. "Kiss-ass," I murmur into her ear.

"At least I'm not afraid of a little dog," she retorts.

That stops me in my tracks. "Little?" I exclaim.

Gemma just shrugs and continues up the porch steps. "Harmless, anyway."

"It's all fun and games until someone gets their head bitten off," I grumble as I follow her.

"You're more likely to get your head bitten off by me." She has the au-dacity to twist around and snap her teeth at me as we cross the threshold into the house. I have a comeback on the tip of my tongue, but Mrs. Dash claps her hands again like a schoolteacher trying to get her class's attention.

"Let's get started, shall we?" She raises her arms and looks around. The space is enormous, with high ceilings and a wrought iron chandelier illuminating the space in warm light. It's dimmer than I'd expect for such a large fixture, and I make a mental note to figure out why that is.

"This is the foyer, obviously," Mrs. Dash is saying. "I'd love to contin-ue the yellow from the outside into this space for continuity."

I bite the inside of my cheek to keep my grimace from showing on my face. "If you're going for brightness," I start carefully, "we could do a lot of whites and creams. Keep it clean and neutral."

"I like color." Mrs. Dash folds her arms. "White isn't a color." She turns and walks further into the house.

"Technically, white is all the colors," I grumble.

Gemma snorts. "When I asked to work with you on this project, I knew you'd be surly, but this is next level."

She follows Mrs. Dash down the hall. I hang back under the guise of tapping out some notes in my phone app, but in reality, I'm floored. My heart skips over itself a few times as I process what I just heard. She *asked* to work with me? Why would she do that?

Her squeal snaps me out of my pondering. "You know what would be perfect in this space?" she exclaims loudly. "A teal retro fridge."

Oh *hell no.*

I bound toward them as quickly as I can, but I'm too late. Mrs. Dash has clasped her hands together and pressed them against her lips in a clear display of ecstatic joy. She looks at me with large, pleading, hopeful eyes. "Please, Mr. Camdon. Can we work that into the design?"

I growl softly and glare at Gemma, who is standing slightly behind Mrs. Dash with her arms crossed and a satisfied smirk on her face. "Oh, Bex can *absolutely* work that in, Mrs. Dash. It shouldn't be a problem at all."

"Wonderful!" she exclaims, then moves away from us into the next room.

Is this why Gemma asked to work with me? So she could continuously piss me off? That would admittedly be more than a little disappointing.

And yet, this teasing is such a far cry from her silent nail-biting in the car on the way here. It's as if she's in her element, talking about project design and client wish lists. Like her work takes some of that anxiety away.

It's almost a relief to see her back to her usual self.

But I can't tell her that. She'd twist it somehow and shoot it back at me or become self-conscious again. So, instead, I say, "You're recycling nicknames, you know."

Gemma shakes her head. "I'm not. That one was spelled with an X. The other was an S."

I reel back, incredulous. "That's a stretch."

She just shrugs and follows Mrs. Dash again. I'm getting a little sick of being left behind, so I march after them.

What follows is a tour of the giant house with the owner telling us all of the things she'd love to see changed. The dining room needs a huge table to seat guests and some other updates. The living room needs a cozier feel, though my eyes catch on the giant fireplace that I'm definitely using as a focal point for the room, and a gorgeous grand piano in the sitting area that is definitely staying. Through the sitting area are an office and a bathroom, both in decent shape.

At every turn, though, Mrs. Dash suggests wild color combinations that have no business being in a home. Gemma, to her credit, doesn't egg her on anymore. Instead, she taps at her phone every once in a while, then asks to see the bedrooms.

Thankfully, Mrs. Dash is open to a more neutral palette for those rooms, as they'll be mostly for bed and breakfast guests. They have clearly not been used in ages, and they have an earthy smell that will need to get aired out.

I glance at Gemma as we close the door to the last bedroom. She taps her phone a few times, then nods to Mrs. Dash. "Do you have a basement?"

"Oh, yes, but it's not livable space. It's completely unfinished," she responds.

"With the extent of the renovations, we'd like to see it anyway, if that's okay? Just to take a look." Gemma smiles reassuringly, and Mrs. Dash nods.

She leads us down two flights of stairs into the basement. It's mostly concrete. I shine my phone's flashlight into the crawl space at the back of it. Gemma pulls a marble from her pocket and puts it on the ground. It slowly rolls all the way to the left before it hits the wall.

That's not good.

"Oh dear," Mrs. Dash says. She must know a thing or two about foundations.

"Not to worry. We'll have the foundation leveled before we start on the remodel," Gemma reassures her.

"This will affect our budget," I say slowly.

Mrs. Dash waves that away. "My late husband left me more money than I know what to do with. Like I told your partner on the phone, there is no budget."

"I'm sure The Beckinator over here will test that statement," Gemma says drily as she sends another text. "One of our guys can come take a look tomorrow, Mrs. Dash. It'll take them about a week, which will likely push our timeline back a little." She chews on a nail as she considers something. "But I can probably make up at least some of the time. Do you have somewhere you can stay while they work? It'll go faster if you're not living in the house with all this going on."

"Oh, yes," Mrs. Dash says. "I was headed to my son's house for Christmas, anyway, and was going to stay until you're done here so I could be out of your hair. I'm sure he won't mind if I come a little early." She tilts her head, then her face lights up like a Christmas tree as she turns her attention to me. "Do you think we could do one of those reveals like they do on the shows? Where you cover my eyes until I'm inside, and then I open them and am just amazed at the work you've done?"

Why on God's green Earth is she asking me this question? Do I look like the reveal type of guy? My gaze shifts to Gemma, who is trying desperately to hold back a laugh. I attempt to convey with just my expression that she should be the one answering this question. When she just shakes her head as her body shudders with repressed giggles, I flash a stiff smile in Mrs. Dash's direction. "Sure."

"Oh, fantastic!" She jumps a little and claps her hands. "Now, let's get out of this creepy basement."

Chapter 6

Gemma

WE FINISH UP WITH Mrs. Dash just before lunch. She tries to get us to stay and eat, but I can tell that Beckett is uncomfortable. As much as I love seeing him squirm, I think I've instigated enough trouble today. I agree to leave, though I'm going to make him stop for a sandwich on the way home.

We say our goodbyes, and Beckett's phone rings loudly as we're getting into the car. It's the old rotary phone ring, which is so *him*, it's almost as if someone scripted it. He slides in behind the steering wheel and answers it without starting the car. I rub my hands together, then slide them under my thighs to ward off the already cold air as I watch Mrs. Dash re-enter her house.

Beckett eyes me sidelong, then says, "Yes. Okay. Great," and hangs up the phone. His head turns slowly in my direction. Those ice-blue eyes bore into me, and a small part of me basks in his singular focus. But the way he's staring at me also makes me very, very nervous.

"When was the last time you changed your fuel filter?" he asks.

"My what?"

"Your fuel filter. In your car."

I frown. "How should I know?"

"You don't know what kinds of routine maintenance you have done on your vehicle and when?"

"Is it routine maintenance to change a fuel filter?"

Beckett drags his hand through his hair that's still more pepper than salt and blows out an exasperated puff of air through pursed lips. "Yes, Woodard. That is routine maintenance."

"Okay..." I say slowly, hunching over and staring out the passenger window. My hand involuntarily finds its way to my mouth again so I can bite the nail on my ring finger. "So, I killed my own car. You don't need to rub it in." I sound like a sullen child, but I don't even care. It's one thing to razz him about his design choices; it's another to make me feel like shit because I can't handle my own life.

"You... what? No." He grabs my wrist and pulls it gently away from me. "Stop doing that. You'll have no nails left."

His hand is so warm and pleasant. It shocks me, because it seems so incongruous with his crusty exterior, and I'm surprised to find I like his touch on my wrist. There's something so kind and reassuring about it. It almost takes some of the tension out of my shoulders. Almost.

I roll my eyes, scrambling to get a handle on my hormones. "Sure, *Mom*."

He regards me for a long moment. Long enough that his expression softens, and I start to get uncomfortable again.

"Why are you looking at me like that?" I ask as I shift in my seat. The leather squeaks under me. Of course it does. Just another reminder of something else I can't afford even in my wildest dreams.

"Your car is fine. My guy just had to replace the filter. We can pick it up on our way back."

I straighten in my seat. "Are you serious?" I ask excitedly, then I slump again when I remember what this is going to do to my wallet. "How much is this going to set me back?"

"Nothing."

I raise my pinched eyebrows, then look at him like he's completely lost it. "What do you mean?"

"I mean," he says carefully, "that it's not costing anything. I told you, he owes me."

"He owes you a last-minute tow, parts, and labor on a car that's not even yours?"

He breathes out a long-suffering sigh. "All tows are last-minute."

I throw my hands up and slap them on my thighs in frustration. "You're not answering my question."

"What's the question?" he asks, equally annoyed.

"I don't believe you!" I cry out.

"That's still not a question."

I glare at him and swallow hard. "I told you before, BK. I can take care of myself."

My relief at being able to come up with another nickname on the fly after almost being caught reusing one is short-lived. Beckett's expression turns soft again, and he tilts his head. "I know you can, Woodard. But does taking care of yourself mean you can never let anyone do anything nice for you?"

I reel back as if he's hit me. "I let people do nice things for me."

"You wouldn't even let me buy you a coffee."

"It was a hot chocolate," I retort, "and I think we both know it wasn't about the beverage. I don't want people paying for my things, especially when they think I can't do it myself. I can."

He studies me again, then nods once and puts the car in reverse to back out of the driveway. Conversation over, I guess. Back to awkward silence while I watch the flat Midwest pass me by in Beckett's fancy-ass car.

Beckett eases onto the country road that will take us to the highway as he says, "I'm not paying for your car. This guy is a buddy of mine. I loaned him some money to start his repair shop." He glances at me, then turns his attention back to the road. "He paid me back, but he does the odd favor for me every now and then. So I called one in. But if your pride won't allow you to accept a kind gesture at Christmas, then it'll probably total around five hundred dollars."

My eyes practically bug out of my head. I can't shell out five hundred dollars if I'm going to be able to buy a house. "Well, if it makes him feel good to do these favors for you, far be it from me to take that away from him."

Beckett hums in an *I thought so* kind of way. It's irritating, but I'm suddenly too tired to engage. The adrenaline I got from giving him crap at the Dash house is wearing off, and the lack of sleep from Nova's wakefulness last night must be catching up with me. It's especially hard to stay awake with the landscape rolling hypnotically by. I settle in for more silence.

After a few minutes, I'm almost nodding off when he says, quietly, "You asked to work with me."

I don't take my eyes off the winter landscape, still too tired to give him shit or lie or even tease. "I did."

"Why?" His voice is gruff, like just asking the question requires a good deal of effort.

I could say something sarcastic about how I love his stubborn ways and his boring neutrals. But what's the point? I'm too drained to even think of a stupid nickname, let alone lie. The truth is, he's not the easiest person to work with, but he's not a bad guy. It's why I started with the nicknames, originally. After I got to know him, pissing him off ended up being a bonus. The other guys in the office all had stupid names they called each other, and he was the only one who insisted on calling me by my last name only. Not "honey," or "sweetie," or worse. I don't know if he respects me—that might be a strong word. But he doesn't demean me, and the more my anxiety has been ramping up, the more I needed this job to be easy.

"Honestly, Beckett? I needed a win before the end of the year, and you're the only guy at the company who doesn't give me crap about my kid or being a woman or a whole host of other probably offensive things about me. So, I thought working with you would be tolerable."

I glance at him out of the corner of my eye, and I could swear I see the corner of his mouth twitch up just a bit. But it lowers just as quickly. "Tolerable," he repeats.

"'Fun' would be a step too far, I think. But yeah."

"You don't have to put up with harassment from them, you know," he says after a pause.

"Yes. I do." I sigh. I don't owe him an explanation, but the angle of his head and the tense grip he has on the steering wheel make me think he's invested in this. Almost like he cares. It makes me want to give him the benefit of the doubt, so I add, "This is what being a woman in a male-dominated profession is like. If I complain, I'm a bitch. If I let it continue, it'll never end. Damned if I do, damned if I don't. I chose a long time ago to let it roll off me. It's easier that way. But you're not like them. You don't really give a shit about much outside of the office. You're happy as long as the work gets done." I reconsider. "Well, happy might be pushing it. But you know what I mean."

"What you're saying is I'm the nice guy in the office."

Is he... teasing? It seems like he is, but his expression is stoic, so it's hard to tell.

"That's not what I'm saying. That's what you're hearing," I correct him. He needs to come down a peg or ten before he lets this get to his head.

"I can be nice," he says softly. "I have even been known to buy a coffee for a coworker on occasion."

I roll my eyes. "Hot chocolate. And I'll never say no to a hot chocolate from a coworker. Just not when he thinks I'm a damsel in distress."

"No," Beckett says, and there's that almost-smirk again. It lights him up, in a way, and I'm shocked to find he's even more handsome when he almost smiles. "You're only a damsel in distress when your car is stalled on the side of the highway."

I flare my nostrils and flatten my lips. Never mind. It's hard to find someone handsome when they're a total asshole.

"I could have called my own help, you know. I'm perfectly capable of using a phone. You were just closer."

"Of course," he says.

I could retort because he's clearly patronizing me, but I don't. The problem is that he's not entirely wrong. So, instead, I let the flat Midwest landscape lull me into relaxation while I try very hard not to think about Beckett's almost-smiles.

Chapter 7

Beckett

THE NEXT MONDAY, I'M sitting in my office with the door open, grumbling over the renderings of the Dash house on my monitor. Not even the gorgeous, instrumental piano versions of Christmas carols playing softly from my computer speakers can save me from the reality that is this kitchen. I had called Mrs. Dash at the end of last week trying to get her to change her mind on the teal retro refrigerator under the guise of the expense and difficulty of finding such a piece. But she simply assured me—yet again—that she has the utmost faith in my ability to find one, and that there is no budget. I suggested a white or even almond design, but she just laughed, told me I was a funny young man, and hung up.

So, now, I'm playing around with a kitchen layout that needs to get done today or else we risk the contractors falling behind schedule, and I'm trying to place a teal refrigerator somewhere that won't look overly garish.

"Oh wow. That's hideous."

I startle in my chair, then swivel it to find Gemma standing behind me, her head cocked and a couple of wayward red curls hanging over her cheek. She's frowning at my computer screen, but from the way her mouth is twisting, it's pretty clear she's holding back a laugh. "Did I scare you?"

"I was working. You should try it sometime," I say drily.

"Hmm," she hums as she cocks an eyebrow. "I have to say, I'm impressed, Becky-pop. I didn't think you had that fridge in you."

I glare at her, wishing I could shoot actual daggers at her across the desk. "You shouldn't have suggested it, then," I grind out.

At that, she does chuckle as she raises her hands, palms out. I hate to admit the sound of her easy laughter does something to my insides that I don't want to think about. I'd much rather go back to shooting daggers in her direction.

"I honestly just said that to fuck with you. I didn't think she'd go for it."

All I can do is blink incredulously at her. "You saw the outside of that house. You heard her say she likes color. And you didn't think she'd want the teal refrigerator you suggested?"

"Okay, I see your point. But it's one thing to like color and another to want an actual teal fridge in your home. That lady is wild." She shakes her head with an appreciative expression on her face. "I kind of want to be her when I grow up."

I frown. "You are a grown up."

She tilts her head back and forth. "Sort of." Then, her expression turns mischievous. "Not as much of a grown up as you, though."

"Are you calling me old?" I ask.

She grins at me, and I want to sink into it, even despite what she says next. "No. Just calling you older than me."

I clear my throat, trying to also clear my head of this nonsense. I don't know where this is coming from, but ever since she slipped and said my full, actual name in the car on the way home from the Dash house, I've had a hard time getting her out of my head. And yet, as she has so clearly stated, she's too young for me. Along with a whole host of other reasons I'd never pursue anything with her.

No matter how pretty she is standing there in a bright green Christmas sweater with curly tendrils of her red hair escaping from the bun piled on top of her head.

I take a deep breath, trying once again to flush my brain of these unwanted thoughts. "Did you need something, Woodard?"

She blinks a few times as if she's also trying to rid herself of similar thoughts. But, no, that has to be wishful thinking on my part.

Get a grip, Camdon.

"Uh, yeah. Mrs. Dash called and said she had stopped by the house this morning to grab a few things she had forgotten since the foundation repair was supposed to be finished and demo was supposed to be underway. Except demo has not started, the electricity is completely out because of some rewiring they had to do, and the place still looks pretty torn up, apparently." She folds her arms across her chest and slides her hands under her arms, squeezing them. The image of her biting her nails in the car comes to mind, and I wonder if she's squeezing her hands to avoid doing it again.

I glance at the kitchen plans on my monitor, but quickly look away from the teal monstrosity taking up a third of my screen. "That's less than ideal."

Gemma nods, worrying her bottom lip. "I'm going to go out there again to check it out myself, I think. The general contractor can meet me on Thursday afternoon."

"The day before Christmas eve?"

She shrugs and drops her hands to her side. "He's not happy about it, but the foundation needs to be finished before we can start demo, and demo needs to happen between Christmas and New Years if we're going to be on track. That foundation put us back already, and I don't want to fall further behind."

Against my better judgement, I glance at my screen and let my thoughts take over. I had my buddy do a once-over on Gemma's car before we picked it up to make sure nothing else would go wrong with it, but after stalling out on the highway last time, I don't love the idea of her driving out there alone again. And I could probably stand to get some more measurements myself instead of relying on the blueprints.

"I'm driving," I say before I can think better of it.

She shakes her head rapidly. "No, I didn't mean for you to have to come with—"

"I need measurements anyway," I cut her off.

She starts biting her full bottom lip again, and I wish she'd go back to biting her nails so I could stop wishing those were my teeth teasing her mouth.

"I can't get a straight answer on what the state of the place is. There's no guarantee you'll be able to get in there for measurements." She's protesting, but it's half-hearted. I don't dare hope that she actually wants my company on this trip.

I shrug. "Worth a shot. Worst-case scenario, I can spend a day *not* staring at a teal refrigerator."

Her teeth release her bottom lip as she smiles, and it feels like a small victory. "Okay," she says. "But I'm buying the hot chocolate."

I nod curtly. "Sounds fair."

She turns on her heel to leave, and I scoot my chair closer to the monitor again so I can figure out where to put this monstrosity, once and for all.

"You're sitting a little close to the screen, old man," Gemma says over her shoulder, her voice a playful singsong. "You might need to think about getting yourself some glasses."

I'm glad she's quickly out of earshot, because I can't help the chuckle that bursts from me, and if she had heard it, she'd never let me live it down.

Chapter 8

Gemma

Not even the all-Christmas, all-the-time radio station can drown out the sound of Beckett's laughter as I walked away from his office yesterday from replaying in my mind. It was a gravelly, rumbling sound that could have melted the frost forming outside the window next to my cubicle.

Who needs hot chocolate when Beckett Camdon has a laugh that sounds like *that*?

"We might actually be in for a white Christmas this year," the D.J. chimes in after a song ends. "Weather experts are calling for a winter storm Thursday evening into Christmas Eve..."

"Want to reschedule the trip to the Dash house?" Beckett's deep voice sounds behind me. He saunters up to my desk and leans a hip against it. I have to physically drag my eyes away from where his ass rests, just out of my reach. When I finally meet his gaze, he's looking at me as if he's waiting for an answer to something, but my mind is blank.

"I'm sorry. What?"

He stares at me as if it hurts him to have to repeat himself. "That winter storm tomorrow might make a drive out to Indiana pretty dangerous."

"Oh," I say, coming back to Earth from my daydream. I glance out the window at the dreary, gray clouds hanging low over the Chicago skyline. "I don't know. They're always screaming about winter weather around here, but nothing ever comes of it. And it's not supposed to start until tomorrow night, anyway. I think we'll be fine." I glance back at him with eyebrows raised. "Why, does winter weather make you nervous?"

He shakes his head. "No." He dips his chin to my hand laying on the desk. "You're the nervous one."

Normally, I'd think he was taking a jab to make me feel shitty about my anxiety. And usually, it would work. But he says it so quietly, so gently, that it's clear he's just looking out for me. Almost like he cares.

That can't be right.

I study his ice-blue stare. His dark eyebrows are pinched, and his eyes are lined with concern.

Maybe it is right. Maybe he just wants to be sure I'm not worried about the winter storm.

I swallow heavily. "I don't think it'll be as bad as they're saying." My voice is surprisingly steady for how shaky he's making me.

He nods, standing. "We can leave mid-morning tomorrow, then."

It's probably my imagination, but he seems to move slightly closer as he walks past me, as if he wants my attention on his ass.

No way. *That* is definitely my imagination.

I try to distract myself by drowning in one of the spreadsheets open on my computer, but it's not long before I see someone else's hands pressed on the side of my desk out of the corner of my eye.

"You've got to stop flirting with the designers, honey," comes a familiar voice. It's low to avoid being overheard, but it unmistakably belongs to Alex Brachs, one of the other project managers.

I grit my teeth and slide my eyes to him. "What do you need, Alex?"

He chuckles darkly, and the sound of it is so different from Beckett's earlier laugh. Alex's sends ice through my veins, and I have to fight a disgusted shiver.

"Nothing. Just wanted to let you know that if you needed someone to trim your tree this year, I'd probably be better at it than Camdon over there." He ticks his head in the direction Beckett went.

This has to be the world's worst euphemism, but I'm not going to give him the satisfaction of opening the conversation to his sexual innuendo. "My tree doesn't need your help," I respond flatly.

Alex's eyes flick toward Beckett's office as he huffs. "I bet it doesn't," he says suggestively. He pushes off the desk, but as he's walking away, he calls back to me louder, for everyone to hear. "Offer stands, though. If you change your mind."

I fight the urge to gag and, instead, switch my music to my earbuds and pop them in my ears. Alex Brachs's ridiculous metaphor isn't anything a little Christmas music can't drown out. But Beckett's words from the other day play over the dulcet tones of yet another Christmas carol.

You don't have to put up with harassment from them, you know.

Usually, it's not that bad. Most often, it's just a diminutive nickname or a pointed question about whether or not I can get something done if I have to leave to get home to Nova. As if some of these men aren't fathers who should also, probably, get home to their kids. But we all know the rules are different for mothers—especially single ones.

This time was more sinister. It leaves me feeling icky. And exposed, I realize as I bring my thumbnail to my teeth. I might not have been flirting with Beckett, but I was checking out his ass, truth be told. Even though I think he might have been flirting with me at times this week, I need to shut that down. The last thing I need is the other guys thinking I'm sleeping around. *They probably already assume I'm easy*, I think as my gaze catches on a framed picture of Nova on my desk.

Nope. I definitely don't need to give anyone around here any more ammo. I just need to get this job done, get out of my parents' house, and give myself a little more breathing room.

Beckett Camdon was barely on my radar before last week, so how hard could it be?

Chapter 9

Beckett

I EASE THE CAR off the highway somewhere in northern Indiana. Gemma has been uncharacteristically quiet again, and it's killing me. So, I take an exit well before the one that would lead us to the Dash house without telling her about it.

It takes her a moment before she notices the detour and finally turns her emerald green eyes in my direction.

"Where are you going?" She sounds a little nervous, and I hate it.

"My buddy told me about a cool coffee shop in this area, and I've been promised some hot chocolate, so I figured we could stop."

"Now?" she asks, her voice squeaky.

I glance sidelong at her. "Is that a problem?"

She drags her bottom lip into her mouth to suck on it as she shakes her head and turns back to her window.

Well, that didn't go the way I thought it would.

As I drive through the streets dotted with wreaths on streetlights and colorful Christmas lights, I try very hard not to look in Gemma's direction. I pull up to the curb and parallel park next to the shop my buddy told me about. The floor-to-ceiling windows reveal a warmly lit and cozy—if not a little old school—coffee shop inside. I exit the car and wait for Gemma to slowly make her way out and to the sidewalk. She looks up at the twinkling lights in the windows, and a ghost of a smile graces her lips.

There it is.

I open the door and motion for her to precede me into the shop. She sheds her gloves as soon as we enter the warm space, and I notice her fingernails are even more destroyed than they were the last time we talked.

People occupy about half the tables in the shop, and no one is behind the counter. But it doesn't take long for a man who looks about my age—though is dressed like a hipster teenager complete with a festive, holiday beanie—to jump up from a table he's sharing with a dark-haired woman and make his way toward us.

"Hi there. What can I get you?" he asks as he dons an apron.

I look at Gemma, who steps up to the counter. "Can I have a hot chocolate, please?"

"Sure thing. Would you like whipped cream on that?"

"Um..." she trails off.

The woman who the barista was sitting with pipes up, flashing a brilliant smile. "I recommend it."

If I'm not mistaken, the man behind the counter flushes slightly as he glares at the woman playfully. I don't know what that's about, but I could guess.

Gemma must also sense the same thing, because she laughs and some of the tension visibly leaves her body. "Sure. Whipped cream would be great."

"And for you?" the man asks, turning his attention to me.

"Same."

Gemma offered me a hot chocolate, and I don't want to disappoint her by ordering something different, even if it wouldn't be my first choice. She smiles softly without looking at me as if she knows exactly why I ordered it, and that might be my favorite smile of hers so far.

She twists her face as she covers her stomach with her hand and looks at the case of pastries. "Maybe a muffin, too?" She looks at me apologetically. "I forgot to eat this morning."

Forgot to eat? I don't like the sound of that one bit. She's going to need more than a muffin if that's the case.

The man at the register nods and punches that in as another man in a crisp, white, button-up shirt and dark slacks comes in from a back room. He looks incredibly put together but is incongruously wearing a Santa hat cocked to the side. "The muffins are amazing," he says as a little girl about Nova's age toddles up to him and crushes his legs in a hug. He picks the girl up and tosses her in the air before setting her down. She squeals in delight and toddles off again. Gemma watches the whole exchange wistfully, hugging herself around her torso. The quiet, swishing sound her thumbs make as they drag back and forth across her jacket fills the air between us for a moment.

"Well, with that endorsement, I'd better get one, too," I say. Gemma gives me a thankful glance, as if she had been embarrassed to eat. Which she should not be.

"I'd ask if you want this for here or to go, but with that storm rolling in, I imagine you want to get where you're going pretty fast," the man says as he puts a couple of muffins in a bag.

Gemma's eyes go wide. "I thought that wasn't supposed to hit us until tonight."

The man shakes his head as he steams some milk. "Last I heard, it's going to roll in about an hour from now. And that lake effect snow is no joke." He eyes us over the retro-looking espresso machine he's using as a steamer.

I vaguely wonder what it is with Indiana residents and their retro appliances before Gemma turns to me, still looking like a deer in headlights. "Do you think we could make it home?"

"Where's home?" the man in the Santa hat asks.

"Chicago," I say. "We were on our way to a home we're renovating about thirty miles east of here."

The barista laughs. "Going west would be a bad idea. You'd be driving right into it. I'd say get some supplies, drive to that house, and plan to spend the night. We're actually closing up here in a few minutes to head out before it starts."

Gemma has gone still. I can almost feel the panic radiating off of her.

I really, really hope that panic isn't because she's going to have to spend the night in the same house as me.

She stiffly hands over her card to pay for the drinks and muffins, then takes her hot chocolate and walks out of the shop as if she's in a daze.

The barista tracks her movements and shakes his head as he hands me the rest of our order. "Good luck, man."

Chapter 10

Gemma

WE'RE ABLE TO STOP at a grocery store and grab some bread, peanut butter, cereal, and a few other snacks to hold us over. There won't be power at the house since it was shut off to do the electrical rewiring, so we can't cook. I haven't allowed myself to think about what sleeping in a house with no heat or power in the middle of a snowstorm is going to be like. My mind is racing, and so is my heart. I can only deal with one step at a time.

While Beckett gets the food, I hang back in the car so I can call my parents, though I don't tell him why. I just quietly ask if he wouldn't mind going in alone, and he doesn't ask questions. I do a video call so I can see Nova's sweet face. She smiles at me and tries to grab at the phone. My parents keep moving it out of her reach as they assure me up and down that she'll be just fine and not to worry at all.

By the time I hang up with them, I'm holding back tears and biting my nails. It doesn't matter how much they tell me not to worry. I've never spent a night away from my baby, and I'm nervous as hell about it.

Beckett comes back holding several paper grocery bags. He slides them into the back seat and wordlessly pulls out of the parking lot. I keep my face turned toward the passenger side window in case I start crying. I don't have a lot of shame about my emotions, but I will *not* have a crying panic attack in front of Beckett Camdon. I can control this anxiety like I always do. I just need a minute.

He takes a breath as if he's going to say something, then lets it out slowly. After a minute or so, he does it again. All of my energy is going toward not breaking down, so I don't have any reserves to worry about what he's trying to say.

When we pull up to the house, it has just started to snow. Big, wet flakes smack against the windshield. My hot chocolate sits in the cupholder to my left, probably cold by now. The bag of muffins is at my feet. I had been starving when I ordered one, but now I feel like I'm going to throw up.

One night. I can make it through one night. Nova is fine. My parents will love the extra time alone with her. It's all going to be okay.

"It's…" Beckett trails off and takes a breath to start again. "I'm not…"

"Spit it out, Kit."

"What?" he asks, confused.

"You've been trying to say something for the past five miles at least. Just say it," I insist, still not turning my face from the window.

"I heard Alex talking to you yesterday. I know it's none of my business but—"

I whip my head toward him at that. "You *what*?"

"He is not a quiet man," Beckett says defensively, and I have to give it to him because that's true. "He's not hard to hear. And I was coming back to your desk with an update about something, so I wasn't far."

I search his blue eyes, trying not to let my hurt show. But the hurt feels good. It feels so much better than the panic that has been creeping up on me since the coffee shop, so I lean into it. "You didn't."

The space between his eyebrows creases. "Didn't what?"

"Come back to give me an update."

"No. I—"

"Because you heard what Alex said," I cut him off again.

The crease between Beckett's eyebrows deepens slightly, then he snaps his mouth shut as if he has just realized why that would be an issue. He heard Alex insinuate I was flirting, which is embarrassing enough, but then he shut me out of a project update because of it. Even though he knows I'm more than capable of doing this job. Even though he's never treated me like that before.

I expect him to say something in his defense, but he doesn't. He just quickly opens the car door and gets out. He grabs the grocery bags and stalks through the falling snow up to the front door. White flakes cling to his wool coat and land in his dark hair as he walks.

Okay, then.

Now, the panic is back tenfold because not only do I have to spend the night away from my baby, but I have to do it with a pissed off Beckett Camdon, who either thinks I was flirting with him or thinks people think I was flirting with him.

I watch him enter the house and flick an internal light switch. Nothing.

Great.

I don't know what I was expecting, but I guess I was hopeful they'd have the electricity back on, at least.

Well, it's more likely that I'll freeze to death in a car buried by snow than in a house, even if that house doesn't have power or heat, so there's nothing left to do but go inside. I loop the handle of the bag of muffins over my forearm and take both my hot chocolate and Beckett's before shoving the car door open with my foot and kicking it closed.

When I get inside the house, Beckett closes the door behind me. It's warmer in here than it is outside without the wind, but not by much. The panicky feeling starts rising in my chest. I can feel my breaths starting to get shorter and shallower.

Not here. I can't do this here. I shove it down as much as I can and walk toward the kitchen so I can set down the things I'm carrying. I hear Beckett's fancy shoes clicking on the tile right behind me.

"Were you?" he asks.

"Was I what?" I say through clenched teeth. I take the muffins out of the bag just for something to do, but I don't think I could eat right now even if I wanted to.

"Flirting."

"Don't flatter yourself," I manage to say. I'm going to lose it. I can feel it. And I'm not going to lose it in front of a coworker. With all this talk about flirting, he already probably thinks I can't be professional. I don't want to prove him right. "Listen, I just... I need a minute, okay?" I don't wait for a response before walking through the living room and sitting room and straight into the first-floor office. I carefully push the door shut.

That done, I lean against the wall and sink to the floor. I pull my knees into my chest and rest my forehead on them. I try to take some deep breaths, but it's hard to breathe around the knot of panic in my throat. What comes out instead are a couple of big, gasping sobs as the tears start flowing.

Chapter 11

Beckett

I AM AN IDIOT. What the actual fuck did I think was going to happen when I brought up Alex's insinuations?

In my defense, I thought it was a good idea at the time. I figured we should clear the air, at any rate. She was obviously nervous, and it seemed like a logical conclusion that it was about me. If she had been flirting, then spending the night here with me could be either embarrassing—if that was all she had intended to do—or a step too far, too fast. I guess it didn't occur to me that she wasn't interested at all.

I really am a moron.

Did I want her to be looking for something more? Yes. I might as well admit that, even if only to myself. I haven't been intentionally flirting with her, but that's probably because I'm just objectively bad at human interaction. I have been looking at her. Thinking about her. And, as long as I'm being honest with myself, wanting her.

But it's pretty clear now that those feelings are not reciprocated. Which should have occurred to me long before I brought it up. She said the guys in the office harass her. I should have put two and two together.

Never mind that their harassment makes my blood boil.

But we have more important things to deal with right now. Namely, that it's freezing in here, the snow is coming down so hard outside I can barely see out the window, and Gemma is in the first-floor office with the door shut. Crying, from the sound of it.

Don't flatter yourself.

Fine. This isn't about me. But then what is it about, and how are we going to survive a blizzard in a house with no power if she won't come out near the fireplace?

I decide to give her some space and text my neighbor to ask him to feed my cat. Then, I get the fire going. When she comes out, at least she'll be warm. Maybe she'll emerge by the time I'm done.

But when the flames are crackling and dancing in the fireplace, she still hasn't appeared. It's getting colder, and I know she hasn't eaten yet. I don't have a choice anymore. I have to check on her.

I stand outside the door for a moment, and all I can hear are big, gasping sobs on the other side.

That's not good.

It doesn't sound like normal crying. It sounds like panic crying, like she's having a panic attack just on the other side of this flimsy door. I want to break it down and hold her until it passes, but I don't think that display of misplaced chivalry will make anything any better.

I settle for tapping softly. "Woodard?" I call roughly. "Everything okay?"

No sooner than it is out of my mouth do I cringe. *No, you idiot. Everything is not okay.* Am I doomed to repeatedly put my foot in my mouth around this woman tonight?

She doesn't answer. The sobs get quieter for a minute, but then I hear her gasping as if she's trying to control it but failing.

I try again. "Can I come in?"

She still doesn't answer, but I hear her shift. The door shakes as if she's pressed herself up against it.

I'll take that as a no.

"I won't if you don't say I can, okay?" I ask as gently as possible. It admittedly sounds less soothing than I'd like, but I'm doing my best. I lower myself to the ground where I imagine she's sitting on the other side of the door and rest my head against it. "Listen, I don't know what's going on, but I can tell you're upset. And I'm very, very bad at small talk, as I'm sure you've noticed."

A wet, huffing sound comes from directly on the other side of the door.

"Was that a laugh? I hope that was a laugh." I mutter the last part. "Anyway," I continue, "if you're upset about being here with me tonight after what that asshole said, you don't have to worry. About me, I mean. I'm not... I won't... shit." I curse softly. I am really mucking this up. What the fuck am I even trying to say?

But then the doorknob twists, and the door pops open. I immediately push it wider and crawl inside. I can see her in the dim light filtering in from the window beyond which the blizzard is officially in full force. She's curled up against the wall, hugging her knees to her chest. Her face is buried, and wild curls the color of dark brick cover her face.

I scoot close enough to her that I can serve as a support, but I'm careful not to touch her. I don't say anything. Just being near her feels like a win for now. Sure enough, her breathing starts to become less ragged.

After a few minutes, she croaks out, "It's not you."

I'm flooded with relief. "Oh." Then, I test the waters. "I suppose I shouldn't flatter myself about that either, then?"

Gemma groans. "That was mean. I'm sorry. When I get..." She pauses, swallowing. "When I get anxious, I get angry sometimes."

I let that settle for a moment. "Is that what's happening? You're anxious?"

She nods.

"But not about being here with me?" I clarify.

She turns her head so her cheek is resting on her knees. Her green eyes are glassy, and they gleam in the dreary light coming through the window. Big, red splotches mar her pale skin, and her makeup is smudged around her eyes.

Still, she's breathtaking. I can't help but feel like it's a privilege to see her this way. Vulnerable. Like she trusts me with her fear.

"No. It's not you. I..." She trails off again. Talking is clearly difficult for her right now, so I wait. "Shit, this is going to sound really stupid when I say it out loud."

"Try me."

Her breathing speeds up again as if she's at war with something inside her mind. "I've never left my baby for a whole night."

She buries her face into her knees and sobs.

I lean over so my head is close to hers. "Gemma," I say softly. I don't think I've ever said her first name aloud before, but I like the feel of it on my tongue. I say it again. "Gemma, can I... Would it help if I held you?" I want to calm her. That's all. Nothing more.

If I keep telling myself that, maybe it'll be true.

"I don't know," she admits between gasps. "I'm not usually near anyone when this happens."

"Can I try?"

"You want to hold me while I panic-cry in a house with no power in the middle of a snowstorm?" Even despite her voice shaking, it still sounds incredulous.

If only she knew. "I really do."

She nods without lifting her forehead from her knees. I close the distance between us, touching our hips together before slinging my arm across her back and shoulders. She immediately folds herself into me, angling her body so she can lean her head against my chest. I rest my back against the wall to give her some more room and weave my fingers into her hair so I can hold her close. It takes all my effort not to moan at the feel of her tucked against my body. She fits so perfectly here.

Which feels like a shitty thing to notice when she's panicking.

"It isn't stupid to worry about your baby, but it's going to be okay," I say into her hair. She smells like cinnamon and sugar. "Is she with someone you can trust?"

She nods against my chest. "She's with my parents."

"Good. They love her as much as you do, I bet. Remind me how old she is?" I know how old her baby is. She turned two in August, and she's adorable. She has dark, straight hair she must have gotten from her father, but big, round eyes just like her mother. But I want to keep Gemma grounded here, and it seems like getting her to talk about her kid is as good a way as any.

Sure enough, I can feel some of the tension seep out of her body. "Two."

"Probably time for a sleepover with Grandma and Grandpa, then," I muse.

"We live with them. For now, anyway."

"So, they already know a lot about her routines, and she's in a place she's comfortable." That's reassuring, I'm sure.

"Yes. That's why this is so stupid. Sometimes I'm not really rational where she's concerned." She chokes back another sob.

Nope, we're not going back there again. I tighten my arm around her. "Still not stupid. You're used to being with her, and you can't be. It's okay to be nervous about that. But she's fine there, and I've got you here. Okay? What's her name?"

She relaxes a fraction again. "Nova. Her dad left me when I found out I was pregnant and said I wanted to keep her. She was a light in the dark for me. So, I named her after this astronomical event that produces a star. It felt fitting."

"That's beautiful," I say as I cradle her upper body. I press my hip closer to hers. "That's really beautiful."

She must be coming down from the adrenaline because she droops into me. For a minute, I think she's fallen asleep on my chest, and even though it's so cold I can see my breath, I'd happily stay right here all night if she'd let me. But her teeth start chattering, and she shudders. That adrenaline crash coupled with the dropping temperature is going to be a recipe for disaster.

Time to get her warm.

"If you feel okay to move, I started a fire in that giant fireplace in the living room. We can sit near it and stay warm. Would that be okay?" I ask, smelling her hair one last time.

She starts to get to her feet, but she's shaky. I jump up next to her and take her hand. I don't know what makes me do it, though I tell myself it's to steady her and not to satisfy my need to continue touching her. She squeezes her palm against mine.

"It seems like you've done this before," she ventures as we make our way to the living room.

"Done what?" I let go of her hand to let her settle herself on the couch. There's a blanket draped over the back of it that I hand to her. She tucks her arms underneath it, still shivering.

"Talked someone through a panic attack." Her eyelids are growing heavy. Hooded, almost, but not with desire. No, that would be my own, I'm afraid.

I blink a few times to clear my expression and sit on the floor so I'm eye-level with her. "Maybe I'm just a decent person?" I try to keep my voice playful. It feels like that's what she needs right now.

She hums, unconvinced. "You don't strike me as that type." Her tone suggests she's teasing, and I purse my lips against a smile. Her eyelids droop some more as she tracks the movement of my mouth.

"I minored in psychology in undergrad," I admit. "It has been surprisingly useful."

Her gaze meets mine again, bright now. "You remember what you learned that long ago?" She beams at her own joke. It changes her entire face, and I'm surprised to find relief, heady and strong, washing over me.

I feel myself break into a smile, but I correct it quickly. "Okay, Woodard. Point goes to you because you look about ready to pass out." I can't help it. I gently tuck one of her curls behind her ear. Her eyelids flutter closed, and she sighs.

"When you wake up, you need to eat something," I insist, but my voice is rough.

She doesn't seem to hear it, though. Or at least she doesn't react. She mumbles an "mmm-hmm" before quickly falling asleep.

I watch her for a long time, the crackling of the fire not nearly loud enough to drown out my thoughts. She's beautiful in a wild, chaotic way. Certainly not the type of woman I ever thought I'd be interested in, but I can't help it. Something about the way she needles me is exciting, and the way she trusted me to hold her through a vulnerable moment sealed the deal. In just a few short weeks, Gemma the Tornado has barreled through the office and into my heart, and I'm pretty sure nothing will be able to stop her from completely destroying me.

Chapter 12

Gemma

It's COMPLETELY DARK WHEN I wake, save for the fire burning brightly in front of me. Beckett is nowhere to be found, but there's a soft piano melody coming from the next room. I wrap the blanket around me and follow the sound.

I have to rub my eyes a few times before my brain registers what I'm seeing. Beckett is sitting at Mrs. Dash's grand piano. And he's playing it quietly. Not only is he playing it, he's actually *good*. Like, really good. And if that weren't shocking enough, he's playing a Christmas song. I didn't think he even liked Christmas.

This man is full of surprises tonight.

I lean against the door frame to watch him. His eyes are closed as if he's fully absorbing the music into his being. He's playing "O Holy Night," but it's so slow and soulful that somehow, despite it being about Christmas, it feels sad coming from him.

The light from the fireplace in the living room bounces off the shiny, black surface of the piano and catches on the silver hairs nestled among the darker ones at Beckett's temple. He almost looks as if he's one with the piano, all polished black and white. He's strikingly handsome like this, his eyebrows pinched together and his body swaying with the melody as his long fingers gently press the keys.

I hold my breath as I watch him and try very hard not to think about those dexterous fingers.

He holds the last chord as if mimicking the breath in my lungs, then releases the keys and places his hands in his lap without opening his eyes. "I hope I didn't wake you," he says after a moment. When his eyes finally open, he finds me immediately.

I shake my head. "That was beautiful," I breathe. "I didn't know you played."

His gaze drops to the keys in front of him as he runs his hands over them lovingly. "My mom insisted I learn. She didn't have a lot of money while I was growing up, but she made me pick one 'cultured' activity, and I thought learning how to play the piano would take away the least amount of time from other things I would have rather been doing." He seems wistful, like it's a good memory. He sighs, looking up at me. "Turns out, I loved it."

"Was it just you and your mom growing up?"

He slides over to make room on the piano bench and pats the space to his left. I cross the room and lower myself next to him, careful not to get close enough to touch.

"Yeah. I don't know much about my dad. She doesn't talk about him, and I never pressed her." He tinkers with a melody, then adds a few chords and finishes with a flourish.

I giggle. "Show off."

He shrugs as his blue eyes meet mine. His gaze is intense and focused solely on me. "I only show off when I have a reason to."

I'm drowning in his eye contact. In him. From this close, I can smell the rosemary notes of his aftershave. All of a sudden, I'm overheated despite the chill this far away from the fireplace. I let the blanket slide off my upper body and pool in my lap.

I swallow hard. "Are you suggesting you have a reason to?"

He tears his eyes away from mine and plays another, spirited melody. My heart skips along with it.

"Maybe," he says when he's finished. "You should eat something."

Even though I could listen to him play all night, just the thought of food gives my stomach other ideas. It rumbles loudly. Beckett shoots me a pointed look.

"Fine." I swipe at my still-sleepy eyes, and my fingers come away dark with runny makeup. I suppress a groan at how awful I must look. "I'm going to... clean up a bit." I take a nearby flashlight with me to the bathroom and pray that the water wasn't also shut off.

When I turn the faucet on and water pours out of the tap, I sigh with relief. It's cold water, but at least I can clean up my face and flush the toilet. I do the best I can in the dim light, then leave the tap dripping to keep the pipes from freezing.

I make my way back to the kitchen to find Beckett smearing peanut butter and jelly on pieces of bread. The plates he's set out already have our muffins from the coffee shop on them, and he arranges the sandwiches carefully next to them.

"Are you a crust person or a no-crust person?" he asks without looking up from his task.

I raise an eyebrow as I sidle up next to him at the counter. "I'm a grown up, so you can leave the crust on."

He's silent and still doesn't look at me, so I say, "Wait. Do you cut the crusts off of your sandwiches?"

"They are objectively disgusting," he responds as he slices the sides off the sandwich in front of him.

"They're the best part," I counter. I grab one of his discarded crusts and pop it in my mouth. "It's where all the nutrients are."

He eyes me skeptically. "That is hippie nonsense."

"It is not," I protest, grabbing another piece of crust and eating it. "That's why it's darker. It's nutritionally different."

He shakes his head incredulously, but even in the dim light, I can see the smirk playing at his lips. It feels like a victory to have made that smile appear.

Beckett scoops up his discarded crusts and deposits them on my plate. And I don't know why, but it strikes me as such a sweet thing to do—to give me more of something I like, even if he didn't want it anyway.

He catches me watching him, and I could swear he blushes, but it's hard to tell when the only light is a propped-up flashlight and an ambient fireplace. After dropping the knife in the sink, which he's also started dripping to prevent freezing pipes, he hands me my plate and waves his hand at two glasses resting on the far end of the counter, each half-full of amber liquid.

"I found a bottle of whiskey in the pantry. I don't think Mrs. Dash will mind, given the circumstances."

I wrinkle my nose. "I'm not a huge fan."

He takes a glass with him and moves toward the fireplace. "You don't have to, obviously. I just thought it might help us keep warm."

I study the glass. On one hand, strong alcohol plus Beckett plus a cozy fireplace is probably going to equal disaster. On the other hand, he has a point.

Ultimately, I take the glass with me. Which, I suppose is a choice on a number of levels.

Beckett has spread a blanket out on the floor next to the fireplace. He's sitting cross-legged in front of his plate, so I do the same across from him.

And then I proceed to practically inhale the sandwich and all the pieces of crust he's made for me. I wash it down with the whiskey, which burns, but is followed by a nice warmth that radiates out from my belly.

When I glance at Beckett, he's sipping from his own glass and watching me, amused. "Would you like another? Or maybe five?"

"Listen, I didn't expect to go almost twenty-four hours without food when I was running late and skipped breakfast this morning, okay?" I glare at him playfully over my glass as I take another sip of the warm liquid. I wince a little as I swallow, but it's actually not so bad once you get used to it.

"Mom life?"

I sigh, breaking off a piece of muffin and popping it in my mouth. "Yeah," I say around my bite. "Even with my parents' help, it's a lot. I don't want to depend on them too much, you know? Especially since I don't plan to be living with them much longer."

"Why not stay with them?" he asks, taking another—much more polite—bite of his sandwich.

"Nova's getting older, and we share a room at my parents'. I want my own space, and I think she needs hers, too. And, I don't know"—I shrug—"it probably sounds stupid, but I want to prove I can do it."

"Seems to be a theme with you."

"Is it so bad to want to live your life on your own terms?" I frown at him as I take another sip of whiskey. It's starting to make me feel all gooey, and I can't say I don't like it.

"I..." he snaps his lips shut and looks as if he's considering something. "No. But I don't think it's bad to have help, either." He nods once as if that's that.

"I'll still have help. I'll just have it my way. My parents are great, but they're always there. I need space."

"For boyfriends?" He studies the fire as he says it, but there's a note of bitterness to his tone.

It might be the whiskey making me bold, but I can't help poking the bear. "What would be wrong about that?"

He takes another bite and follows it up with a sip. "Nothing."

"Doesn't sound like nothing, Becker."

Why am I doing this? Why am I instigating? I know well enough that grumpy Beckett Camdon is a loner and a scrooge, and any interest he may have shown in me is either fleeting, out of common human decency, or a figment of my imagination. I shouldn't let it go to my head just because he hugged me a few hours ago, and I certainly shouldn't let my hormones talk. It's not on him that I've been practically celibate since Nova was born.

But, for some reason, I can't help myself. Maybe it's boredom or the whiskey or the way his ice-blue eyes are focused on me, as if drinking me in is warming him more than the whiskey.

"What?" I ask, after he's been silent for a while.

"Were you flirting with me?" He spits out the words like he's worried if he doesn't, he'll never say them.

"Trust me, Beecher. You'd know if I was flirting with you." I cock an eyebrow and take another drink, only to find it empty.

"Like now?" he asks, and I'm pretty sure I detect hope in his voice.

"It's inappropriate to flirt with coworkers. Especially ones with fancy salaries and offices."

"Only if it's unwelcome," he fires back.

Well, I wasn't expecting that.

"Are you saying you want me to flirt with you?" I draw the words out slowly in disbelief.

He shakes his head. "I'm *saying* I wouldn't take it up with HR." He quickly swipes my empty glass from where it sits next to me and stands. "I'm going to need another drink," he grumbles on his way to the kitchen.

Yeah. Me too.

Chapter 13

Beckett

I'M WALKING A TIGHTROPE here. On one hand, I know that getting involved with this woman is going to make everything all kinds of complicated. On the other, I have never wanted anything in my life more than I want to taste her bottom lip as I draw it between my teeth.

Get a fucking grip, I tell myself as I pour two more glasses of whiskey. I eye them, take a large gulp of mine, then fill it a little more so it's even with hers again.

When I rejoin her, the whiskey is starting to steady me. But she looks up at me with those fucking gorgeous green eyes, and you better believe I make damn sure my fingers brush against hers as I hand her the glass. The crimson color that rises on her cheeks is unmistakable even in the light of the fireplace.

I sit down, closer to her this time, and her lips part on an inhale as she turns to face me. I have as much resolve as any man, but she is testing it when she gives me looks like that.

"Jacob doesn't pay you a salary?" I ask. I know full well he does, but I'm scrambling for a more neutral topic of conversation.

She blinks a few times, confusion evident in her features, but she recovers. "He does, but it's small. I make bonuses on each project I complete. He doesn't talk to you about the business?"

I shake my head. "He offered to make me a partner years ago, but I declined. I just want to design. That's why I left my corporate job. To get back to what I love doing." I study her for a moment as I consider what I'm about to say. "You want to get out of your parents' house, so you needed this project because of the bonus. That's why you wanted to work with me."

She averts her gaze. "I already told you. I wanted to work with you because most of the other guys treat me like shit."

"And you wanted an easy project." I can't stop the disappointment from seeping out into my words. I don't know what I was hoping for. That she has harbored a secret crush on me since the start? Of course not. But it doesn't stop the pang from hitting me straight in the chest.

"What were you expecting?" She echoes my thoughts. "You've never been particularly nice to me. I wasn't dying to work with you, either. But you're a decent man, Beckett. The more time I spend with you, the more I wouldn't mind working with you again, for better reasons next time."

It's not the first time she's used my full name instead of one of her stupid nicknames, but the sound of it goes straight to my dick. All I want is to hear her moaning it as I bury my head between her exquisite thighs. I adjust my legs so she can't see what she's doing to me.

"What about now?" I find myself asking. "Are you enjoying this as much as I am?"

That was a little more forward than I meant to be, but it's out there now. We lock eyes for a heartbeat, and it's the longest moment of my life before she slowly nods her head. "I'm glad I'm stuck here with you."

The corners of my lips tug up into a smile, and hers follow. It's like our lips are attached by strings, the way one smile begets the other.

"I'm not too old for you?" I tease.

"I'm not too much of a mom for you?" she counters.

I huff a quiet laugh. "I suppose we both have baggage."

She folds her arms, which really just accentuates her chest, and I'm glad I moved my legs. "I consider mine a strength, not a weakness," she insists.

"Mine, too." My voice is low and husky. I'm doing a very bad job of hiding how much I want her.

She blushes again but doesn't break eye contact with me. "How so?"

"You call it old. I call it experienced."

"As long as we're stuck here..." she trails off and drops her gaze to the glass in her hands. She visibly steels herself and looks me in the eye again. "You should prove it," she taunts. And then she fucking licks her lips as if she knows what's coming. As if she wants it.

I carefully set my glass down out of the way, slowly so she can't see my hands shaking. I breathe deeply, then take hers from her and do the same. "Just as long as we're stuck here," I say. "Just tonight."

Her breath hitches, and her eyes go wide, but she doesn't look nervous. She looks excited. Anticipatory. Like she wants to scream, *holy shit, this is actually happening.*

"I think we owe it to ourselves." Her voice is surprisingly calm. "Considering all the flirting."

"We should get it out of our systems, probably," I agree.

"Exactly." She leans forward slightly, her eyes dark with desire.

I slowly brush her curls away from her face, scanning every inch and counting every freckle. No need to rush. We have all night for this, and if I can only have one night with her, I plan to take my time.

Her eyelids flutter closed, and she breathes in deeply. I trace my finger gently along her jaw, and she exhales a little whimper.

"You can keep those pretty eyes closed for now, Gemma," I whisper, "but I want to see them open and watching me later."

She gasps, and her eyes fly open. "Oh my god," she moans. "Are you serious?"

I chuckle. "Not a fan of dirty talk?"

She swallows hard and shakes her head. For a moment, I'm pretty sure I fucked up by hitting the gas too fast, but she practically melts into the contact my palm is making with her cheek and breathes, "I'm very much a fan, but... say my name again."

"Gemma," I whisper, then lean in.

Chapter 14

Gemma

HIS LIPS ARE FEATHERLIGHT on mine. It's the barest brush, like he's taunting me. I remain unmoving, letting him take the reins. Just like when he held me in the office earlier, it feels so good to let him be in control for a minute. To let him in.

Even the skim of his lips sends a fire through me. The layers of clothes and jackets we left on to ward off the chill are now way too thick.

His fingers curl into my hair, and he angles my head as he pulls slightly away. My eyes flutter open as I frown at him.

That's it?

He looks almost pained. Tortured. Like that wasn't enough for him, either. But he searches my face for something and asks, "Are you sure about this? Because if I start kissing you, I don't think I'll be able to stop."

"You won't be able to stop kissing me? Or you won't be able to stop yourself from going further?" I intend to tease him with this question, but my voice is low and raspy. I think it's probably pretty obvious what answer I'm looking for.

"You're in charge here, Gemma," he says, and my breath hitches when he uses my name again. "But I would very much like to explore the second option."

"Just for tonight," I repeat, as if saying it again could make me believe it.

Beckett huffs, and for a second, I think he's going to tell me he wants more than just one night. Instead, he whispers, "Well, maybe the morning, too."

A whimper escapes me all on its own, and Beckett smirks at the sound. I haven't wanted anyone in a long time—not the way I want Beckett right now. I want to drag my fingers through his salt-and-pepper hair and hold on tight as he presses himself inside me. I want to see what he can do with all that experience he boasted about a few minutes ago.

But I don't know. He's a coworker. And until very recently, I'm pretty sure he's hated my guts. Not to mention that *technically*, he's a rung or two above me on the office hierarchy. So, no. I definitely can't.

Can I?

Desire is plainly written on his face, too—from his hooded, dark eyes to the gentle part of his lips and his shallow breathing. I don't think anyone has ever looked at me like that before.

There's no harm in this if he wants it as much as I do, right?

Ugh, I just want to turn my brain off for one damn second. It feels constant. A never-ending freight train of questions and worries and trying to be perfect all the time and inevitably fucking everything up anyway. Why can't I just let go and enjoy wanting someone who so clearly wants me?

Beckett pinches his brows as if he's watching this war play out over my features, which is decidedly the least sexy thing on the planet.

It's probably now or never.

"You know what?" I mumble. "Fuck it."

I practically leap at him, wrapping my arms around his neck and my legs around his torso. Our lips crash together on a grunt and an exhale.

I had worried about whether or not Beckett wanted this, but I shouldn't have. He is an entirely willing participant in this make-out session, as evidenced by the bruising way he devours my mouth. This kiss is all tongue and teeth, and when he draws my bottom lip in, I groan.

My skin is burning. I may as well have jumped into the fireplace. Every inch of me is simultaneously boiling and crying out to be touched. I tug at the zipper of my jacket and shrug out of it, then get to work on the buttons of Beckett's wool coat.

He lets me work clumsily at the buttons while his hands slide up my back, under my shirt. His palms are warm and calloused, and they leave a tingling trail in their wake.

He feels so damn good between my legs. I squeeze my thighs tighter around his torso and press myself closer to him. The hard outline of his cock meets my aching core, and I tip my head back, completely lost.

It's as if the soundtrack of racing thoughts has scattered, and I can breathe again. And when Beckett presses a hot kiss to my neck, my body responds without much input from my mind. I grind my hips against him, chasing a pleasure that's just out of reach.

"Is it too forward if I tell you I want the rest of these clothes off of you?" he asks into my skin.

I move my hips back and forth, and the motion pulls another moan from him. "The feeling is mutual."

He leans backwards so he can access the button on my jeans. "I didn't plan to have sex with you tonight, Woodard." His voice is tinged with the slightest bit of regret. "I don't have a condom with me."

That doesn't stop him from pulling himself out from under me and dragging my jeans down my thighs. The chilled air hits my skin, and I'm a live wire of sensations. My legs are still spread in the absence of his body, and he looks wantonly at my cotton panties.

What did he say? Oh, right. Birth control. "I have an IUD." I bite my lip. "And I'm clear." I don't mention I haven't been with anyone since Nova was born. He doesn't need that sad piece of information.

He runs his hands up the sides of my thighs and cups my ass. "I'm also clear." His eyes meet mine with an intensity that takes my breath away. "In about five seconds, I'm going to rip these panties off of you. But you say the word, Gemma, and we stop. Okay?"

Who needs a Christmas gift when Beckett Camdon is saying words like *that* and promising to unwrap *me*?

"Okay," I whisper, and that's all he needs. He fists my panties where his hands are on my ass and pulls them off in one swift movement. His palms quickly meet my inner thighs, and he presses my legs further open. The cold air meets my warm core. I shiver slightly, though I'm not sure if it's because of the chill or the way Beckett is looking at me as if I'm a Christmas feast laid out for him.

"Fuck, you're pretty," he mutters. "I want these gorgeous thighs wrapped around my ears until you come, do you understand?"

I'm having a hard time catching my breath, but I manage to choke out, "Yes."

"Good." He flattens his stomach against the blanket and shimmies himself so his mouth is so close to my pussy, I can feel his breath on it. My body is buzzing with anticipation, but I remain completely still, waiting for his next order.

"Take off that sweatshirt and lay back," he commands. I quickly discard my shirt and press my back flat against the floor. I roll my head so I can see him. He cups his hands under my knees and brings them up around his shoulders. "Remember what I said, Woodard. Wrapped around me until you can't remember your own name."

I squeeze my inner thighs around his head, and he groans his admiration before he licks straight up my center, and stars light up my vision like Christmas lights. It has been so long since anyone has touched me like this, but something about Beckett's ministrations feels different. Special. Like he wants nothing more than to be lapping up my arousal on the floor of an old house in front of a fire.

My eyes are squeezed shut, and my head has lolled back so I'm facing the ceiling when he presses one of his long fingers inside me, then another. He flicks my clit with his tongue a few times while he draws his fingers in and out of me. I press my feet into his back and buck my hips into him almost involuntarily.

My hands need somewhere to go, so I bring them up to my tits and roll my nipples between my fingers. Beckett pushes another finger into me, and I cry out at the exquisite pressure of it.

"You are a fucking treat, Gemma." His voice rumbles against my skin. "I can't believe I get to see you like this."

"Oh my god, Beckett," I pant. "I can't... I'm going to—"

"Fuck my face until you come, baby. I can take it."

I weave one of my hands into his silky hair and hold on while I meet his tongue with my hips and let the pressure build and build. For one moment, I wonder if this is okay for him. As if he's reading my mind, he moans and presses his tongue harder against my clit. It's so responsive—so intimate—that it shatters me into a million tiny pieces.

Chapter 15

Beckett

WHEN GEMMA COMES ON my tongue, she tastes like fucking bliss. Everything about her is gorgeous as her orgasm rocks her body. Her pussy clenches and unclenches around my fingers, and I continue to thrust them in and out of her to prolong her pleasure.

There's something so validating about giving a woman this release, especially one as tightly wound as Gemma. I wouldn't mind doing it again. And when I draw my fingers out of her and she props herself up on her elbows to look down her naked body at me, I can't stand not being near her.

I hope she knows I'm just getting started.

I quickly shed my own clothes as she watches, her gaze heating again as she drags her sparkling green eyes down my body. When they come to rest on my dick, she pulls her swollen bottom lip through her teeth. My cock bounces as if it's preening at her attention, and she smiles. I close my fist around it and pump a few times, unable to tear my own gaze away from her flushed skin and her legs still waiting open for me.

Her head drops backwards, and she moans loudly. It's a greedy, impatient sound. "I wish I could get off on watching you look at me like that, Ketty, because it's really fucking hot."

"Correct me if I'm wrong, but you already got off once this evening."
I pump my cock again as she raises her head to watch.

"Mmm-hmm," she hums, her hooded eyes tracking the movement.
"And I'd like to do it again."

Her surety that she can—and will—makes me impossibly harder, and
I'm hoping that my enthusiastic participation in this is implied, because
I cannot imagine not being buried in her. Immediately.

I sit between her legs and drag a finger through her center. She's still
so wet for me. I quickly grab under her knees and pull her ass into my lap
so my cock pushes against her clit. She braces her hands behind her and
uses the floor for leverage as she grinds against me, her wetness making
me slick. Before I can think too much about it, I adjust her so I can slide
inside. She's so wet, all it takes is one thrust and I'm fully seated.

"Oh my god, Beckett," she breathes, pitching forward so she's hugging
me. Her legs wrap around my torso again as her heels dig into my back.
This has the effect of bringing me even further into her, and she gasps.
"Shit. I..." She buries her face in my neck. "Go slow, okay? It's... been a
while."

I'm going to have to go slow or I'm going to blow it right now, but I
don't tell her that. I cup her chin with my hand and make her look at me.
When our eyes meet, there's barely an inch of space between our faces.
Her breath smells of whiskey and is coming in quick gasps, though not
the panicked ones from earlier. These are gasps of someone on the edge,
trying to hold on.

"Tell me if you want me to stop, or if you don't like something, okay?"
I say again. I don't want her getting hurt in an effort to give me what I so
obviously want.

She nods as she bites her lip and closes her eyes. She rocks against me,
and my fingers tighten against her chin. Fuck, she feels so *good*.

Suddenly, Gemma rolls her hips again as she dips her chin and sucks my finger into her mouth. "Oh, shit," I curse as she swirls her tongue around the tip of it. She must be able to taste herself, and she groans with pleasure as she laps it up off my finger.

This woman is so fucking hot. I need to get a grip if I want this to last.

I start to meet her hips with shallow thrusts of my own, and her head falls backwards, giving me a perfect view of her neck. I trail a wet finger down it and over her torso. Her stomach muscles clench beneath my touch. I flatten my hand against the flesh there, and her head snaps up, her eyes wide.

"I'm sorry," she whispers. "That's my least favorite part of me." She lets out a self-deprecating laugh.

I bring my hands to her sides and dig my fingers in as I pull her closer to me once, twice more. "Why?" I grind out. "You're gorgeous." I meet her hips with mine again. "Every inch of you. Now put your hands behind you again so I can see your perfect tits bounce while I fuck you."

"You sure know how to treat a lady," she jokes, but she does as she's told. I'm rewarded with the rebound of her breasts when I thrust again.

"I was informed you like a little dirty talk," I counter.

"Oh, I do." She pushes against her hands to take me harder, and I match her force. "But I also like giving you shit."

"Mmm," I hum. "Let's see if I can get you to forget how to talk trash for a while, shall we?" I drag one hand down her body and cup between her legs. Gemma lets out a huge, gasping moan when my fingers meet her clit. I start making small circles against her. She bucks her hips wildly in time with my movements.

I might have joked about shutting her up, but words are completely failing me now, too, as our bodies move in time with one another. I'm so close, but I clench my jaw and try to hold out. Luckily, I don't have to wait long.

"Beckett," she breathes. "I'm going to…"

"Yes, baby. Come for me again." I make another small circle with my finger. "I'd like to come inside you if you'll let me."

She nods vigorously, then cries out, her body shaking and her pussy clenching me tighter, deeper. One more pulse, and I'm spilling into her, our bodies slick and sticky with cold sweat and sex.

After a few minutes, when we both come down, she slides off me and wraps my coat around her. She swipes a flashlight off the ground where she left it and pads on bare feet to the bathroom. The floor is freezing, I notice, so I lay a blanket out as close to the fire as is safe. I get another two blankets and set them up like a makeshift bed for us to sleep on. I hope she'll let me sleep near her. At the very least, our combined body heat should keep us warm along with the fire.

When she comes back from the bathroom, she stands in the doorway, eyeing my setup. "Are you going to say that cheesy line from the movies about body heat keeping us warmer?" She cocks an eyebrow.

"Absolutely not," I say drily. I hope it doesn't give away that she's called me out. "What part of me suggests I'd ever use a cheesy movie line on you?"

She narrows her eyes at me, clearly skeptical. "You… want to sleep together, though?"

I shrug a shoulder, trying to appear nonchalant. "We have to sleep in the same room, anyway. And our body heat might be helpful, now that you mention it." The corner of my mouth tips upward completely against my will. I purse my lips against it, but by Gemma's wry smile, she saw it.

She puts her flashlight-free hand on her hip, and I'm suddenly very jealous of that hand and my coat as it presses against her skin. "Beckett Camdon," she mock-scolds. "Did you just make a joke?"

"Wouldn't dream of it." I slide under the blankets and pat the area next to me. "You coming in or what?"

That wry smile stays right where it is as she opens my coat and lets it pool at her feet. I curse the fact that I'm not twenty anymore because I would take her again right now if I could.

Hopefully, she's okay with quality over quantity.

She saunters over to me and lowers herself onto the floor. She lies down with her back to me and wiggles around, trying to get comfortable on the hard surface. Once she settles, I lie on my back, near to her but not touching. We said we just wanted to get it out of our systems. I want to be respectful of her if I'm out of hers. But she's far from out of mine, and I doubt I'll get much sleep tonight.

Enough time passes in silence that I think she's fallen asleep, but then she takes a sharp inhale. "Do you..." She trails off and grunts in frustration. "Do you want to hold me?" Then, she adds, "You might be right about the body heat."

I chuckle and narrowly avoid blurting out that, fuck yeah, I want to hold her. I roll to my side, pulling her so the silken skin of her back is pressed up against my chest. She weaves her legs into mine and presses her cold feet to my shins. I slide my arm under her head to give her my bicep as a pillow. She sighs contentedly and melts into me as my other arm encircles her waist even tighter.

It's not long before we're both drifting off, snuggled together and as warm as we can get. My last thought before completely giving into sleep is that I could get used to being pressed up against Gemma Woodard just like this.

Chapter 16

Gemma

BECKETT MUST HAVE GOTTEN up sometime in the middle of the night to tend to the fire, because when I wake up with a crisp, blue, winter sunrise shining in my face from the living room window, the fire is still roaring, and we're no longer entwined like we were when we fell asleep.

Light snoring comes from behind me, and I slip out from under the blankets as carefully as I can so as not to disturb him. I throw his coat around me and tiptoe over to the counter where I had left my phone last night. Beckett must have powered it off for me, because nothing happens when I tap it. That was smart, considering there's nowhere to charge it. And kind. And thoughtful.

It's been a minute since someone thought to do something small and meaningful for me. At least, that's what I tell myself when tears prick my eyes, because it's silly to be emotional over someone looking out for me in this way. I'm usually the one who has to be in charge of all of the things, looking out for everyone else. Even living with my parents—they love Nova and me and are always willing to jump in to help, but they don't generally take care of small things like this. It's not that they don't want to. That's just not how we operate.

I power on my phone and quietly move to the office, shutting the door softly behind me. As soon as my phone lights up, I video call my mom. She answers on the first ring.

"Hi sweetie," she says as her smiling face fills the screen. She pulls the fluffy edges of her robe closed tighter. Her image jostles as she props the phone up on something in front of her. "It's good to see your face. That storm was pretty intense."

"Are you all okay?" I try to keep my teeth from chattering in the cold away from the fireplace and Beckett's warm body. And then, I try to keep the flush from rising in my face at the thought of Beckett, naked under the blankets in the next room.

"It wasn't as bad here as it was where you are. Your dad was watching the radar all night. Most if it missed us and hit you, he thinks."

Of course he was watching the radar all night. Checking the weather and playing amateur meteorologist during a storm is peak Midwestern Dad. And if you looked up that term in the dictionary, there would be a picture of him right next to the definition.

I grin at that, even as I glance out the window to see nothing but giant, white piles of snow as far as the eye can see. "Yeah," I sigh as my mood drops. "I don't know when we'll be able to get out of here. I think Beckett's car is probably buried."

"That's okay, Gemmy. As long as you're safe. Nova is fine with us. She's actually still sleeping." Mom is trying to be reassuring, but my damn tears are starting again.

"It's Christmas Eve, though." My voice is pitiful and small. "I love Christmas Eve with you."

"I know, honey. But we can have a redo of Christmas if we need to, as long as you're safe," she repeats, sterner this time. I know she's right. We were lucky to make it here before the storm, and even though it's cold, we have a fire and food. Things could be worse.

"I didn't get her a present yet," I whisper as I wipe at my eyes. "I was going to do it last night when we got back."

Mom tilts her head to the side. "You've been so busy with this job, Gemmy-bear." It's not scolding. She's offering me an explanation, but the guilt creeps in, nonetheless. "Nova's so young. She won't remember. Just focus on getting home as safely as you can, okay? We can worry about the rest later."

I nod silently and swipe tears away from my eyes again. "Give Nova a big squeeze for me, okay? I should probably go and save my phone battery."

"Of course, honey. We'll see you soon."

We say our goodbyes, and I take an extra few seconds after I turn off my phone again to collect myself. When I think I've shoved my sadness down far enough that it'll stay put, I leave the office and make my way back to the warmth of the living room.

I try to slide back under the covers carefully, but as soon as I'm nestled in, Beckett rolls to me and wraps his arm around my torso. He presses a hot kiss against the back of my neck.

"How's Nova?" he asks.

"Sleeping," I reply simply. "Sorry if I was loud."

"You weren't. I guessed you'd call her first thing."

That tugs at my heart, too. Since when does he know me so well?

It doesn't seem like something that requires a response, so I don't say anything. Instead, I concentrate on breathing steadily, trying to enjoy Beckett's skin pressed up against mine.

"What's wrong?" he asks after a while. "Aside from the obvious not being with your daughter on Christmas Eve."

"Well, that. Mostly." I admit. "But I didn't get a chance to get her Christmas present. I was going to do it yesterday but..." I trail off and shrug as best I can in Beckett's embrace. "She won't remember it anyway, I guess."

"Yeah, but you will," he says softly.

Well, fuck. This man is bound and determined to make me cry again, isn't he?

"I will." I stare at the flickering flames in front of me and pray the tears won't start. "But I can deal with disappointment."

"Doesn't mean it's not still upsetting for you." He squeezes me tighter, and it feels so damn good. I could get used to having someone take some of the weight off. Someone like Beckett who seems to understand how crushing the pressure is sometimes. But I don't dare get my hopes up that this is any more than a one-time thing. Snowed-in sex at Christmas isn't meant to be the foundation for a lasting relationship.

Sure enough, Beckett scoots closer to me, his hardness pressing up against my ass. I giggle. It should feel crass, but that takes some of the pressure off, too. It's almost like he knows I need to get out of my own head for a while, and he's providing assistance.

"I'm sorry." He doesn't sound at all sorry. "I can't help it. You're gorgeous." His hand starts inching upward toward my chest. It's achingly slow, as if he's giving me a chance to shut him down.

I grab his hand with mine and press it against my breast where his fingers immediately cup around it. As he plays with my nipple, I press my ass cheek against his cock so he can grind against it, which he does with a low moan.

He drags his hand away from my swollen nipple to cup between my legs. When he presses two fingers inside me and palms my clit, I cry out.

"Fuck, yes." I'm panting already.

Beckett kisses my neck, and I tilt my head as much as I can to give him access. The pace of his hand is slow and steady, and he matches the thrusts of his palm to the thrusts of his hips against my ass. Where last night was needy and hungry, this morning is sensual and passionate. Is he is thinking about this being more than just snowed-in sex, too?

But I'm going to have to unpack that later, because I'm desperate for more than just his hand between my legs.

I grab his wrist as a signal for him to remove his fingers, which he does. I lift my top leg higher, and before I can tell him what I want, he grabs underneath my knee and his cock presses against me just shy of entering.

"Is this what you want?" Beckett whispers in my ear.

"Yes." I swallow hard in anticipation as I try to lower myself onto him, but his hand tightens around my leg, keeping me in place.

He presses about an inch into me. Not nearly enough. Then pulls out. I whimper in protest.

"How badly do you want it?" he teases.

I moan. "You're not going to make me say it."

The tip of him enters me again, then he pulls it out. He pushes forward so his cock grazes against my clit. I squeeze my eyes shut and gasp.

"I'm absolutely going to make you say it. How much do you want me inside you, Gemma?" His voice sounds like chocolate, molten and gooey and full of pleasure.

"Right now," I pant, "I want you inside me more than I want anything else in the entire world."

He enters about an inch again but doesn't pull back out this time. "How much of me do you want?"

"All of you," I respond without hesitation.

"Are you sure?" His cock goes just a little further inside of me. I'm pretty sure I'm going to explode.

"God, yes. Please, Beckett."

And then, he's fully inside me. I breathe a sigh of relief at being filled with him again. I hadn't realized how much I missed it in the few hours we had been asleep.

"You said the magic word." His teeth graze the skin of my neck. I shiver.

"What, 'please?'"

"No." His cock pulses inside me. "Beckett."

He starts a rhythm with his hips that he matches with his hand that was holding my leg up. In its absence, I rest my leg on top of his, which has the effect of squeezing me tighter around him. I can feel him even better inside me. "Beckett," I call on a moan. "Keep doing that, and I'll say your name as many times as you like."

"Not good enough." He thrusts harder. I'm so hungry for it that I loop my leg around his and push myself even closer. "My name is going to be the only one you remember when I make you come so hard you see stars."

"Mmm-hmm," I agree, because he's right. I can't think of anything but him. He surrounds me. The heat of his skin, the rosemary scent of his aftershave, the raspy and desperate sound of his breath in my ear. He blocks out everything else. He's everything I never knew I needed.

He snakes his other hand underneath me and uses it to pinch one of my nipples. It's sensory overload, but in the best way. It's pain and pleasure and impulse and understanding all rolling me into a tight little ball of desire. The pressure builds in my core as Beckett finds the perfect rhythm behind me.

I'm going to snap, and soon. "Oh," I breathe. "I'm close."

"Me too. You're so fucking pretty when you come, Gemma. Let me see it."

His fingers move faster over my clit, and the pressure inside me splinters. I shudder and pulse and cry out his name over and over again. His tempo becomes completely erratic as he thrusts impossibly deeper and harder. It only strokes the sensitive parts inside of me more, and I continue to shake with my release. He buries his head in my neck as he pulses one more time, then comes inside me.

We lay there until long after he's softened. The fire is dying, and the cold sunlight streaming through the window signals it's closing in on noon. With each passing moment, my hope that we'll get plowed out in time to make it home for Christmas Eve dwindles like the flames. I know I should clean myself up, maybe even put some distance between Beckett and me because it's going to have to happen eventually. But it feels too good, laying here, his fingers stroking up and down my side, his lips pressing against my neck and back every so often.

I'm almost nodding off when an extremely loud, scraping noise comes from outside. Beckett's hand on my side stills as we listen.

That sound is unmistakable. It's a plow.

I sit up with a gasp, almost giddy. "Is that what I think it is?"

Beckett is slower to drag himself off the floor, almost as if he's sad to leave our cocoon behind. "I suppose it's a Christmas miracle," he intones. Funny, that doesn't sound like he thinks it's a miracle. He starts pulling his clothes on, and I have to admit, when I see him doing that, I'm not sure I think it's much of a miracle, either.

"Why don't you get cleaned up. I'll see what's going on," he suggests. I nod and gather my clothes on my way to the bathroom.

Chapter 17

Beckett

I TRY TO FIND an ounce of shame for the way I ogle Gemma as she hurries to the bathroom, but I have none. Her ass is perfect. I'm only a little shocked at the revelation that I would like to look at it every day.

The plow outside scrapes against the pavement again, and I'm quickly reminded that this situation between us is about to end as soon as we leave this house. I'm sure she doesn't want to carry any of what happened over the last twenty-four hours outside of here. The guys at the office already give her enough shit; she doesn't need them thinking she's getting special treatment because she's with me on top of it. I don't even know if she *wants* to be with me, or what "with me" looks like. She's got a kid, for crying out loud. I can't just waltz into her life like there aren't any repercussions if things don't work out.

This is a mess. And I don't do messes. I do white walls, clean lines, and a nice, quiet Christmas.

For a minute this morning, when I was awake and rekindling the fire, I looked outside and figured there was no way we'd be getting out of here before tomorrow. I had visions of whiskey and peanut butter and Gemma's luscious curves dancing in my head. But this plow is clearing those away with the snow, and it's turning everything sour.

I pull my clothes on with more force than absolutely necessary and head outside before Gemma leaves the bathroom. Maybe the fresh air will do me good.

"Morning!" a young man shouts as he jumps down from his truck. There's a plow attached to the front of it, and he's holding a shovel in his hand. "I'm Jack."

"Beckett," I reply, shielding my eyes against the harsh, winter sun bouncing off the bright snow. "My... coworker and I got stuck here last night. We're working on renovating the house."

"Ah," Jack says as if this explains something. "I knew this wasn't Mrs. Dash's car, but I thought maybe her son bought a new one and was visiting for Christmas or something. I hadn't heard she was renovating."

It's clear this man wants to chat with me, and I don't do chats, so I shrug. "Well, she is."

"Makes sense. Mr. Dash left her a lot of money, and this place could use an update." Jack whistles approvingly. "She hires me to do odd jobs every so often. That's why I'm here. I always plow the road and dig out her car after a storm," he says by way of explanation. "And, you know, to check up on her. It's the neighborly thing to do, right?"

"Right." I jam my hands in my pockets. Jack finally stops talking and clears enough of a space behind my car that I'll be able to back out of the driveway and onto the one lane of freshly-plowed country road.

I should be grateful. This way, Gemma and I won't be able to get in any deeper or make things any messier. I can go back to my condo, check on my cat, and pour myself some brandy. Like I always do on Christmas Eve. Who cares if my fireplace is gas-powered and chic, not the huge wood-burning hearth Gemma and I made love in front of. Twice. It's for the best, probably, because then I won't be reminded of the way her skin felt against mine, or how my heart felt funny when she repeatedly called out my name.

As if thinking of her summons her, the screen door behind me bangs, and she comes up next to me. Her scent envelops me—all spice and sugar.

Jack pauses in the process of loading his shovel into the back of his truck. "Mornin', Miss," he says. "I was telling your coworker here, I always come plow Mrs. Dash's route after a storm like this. I wasn't sure she'd be here or with her son, but I saw your car and figured you could use some help getting out of here."

She seems to tense at the word "coworker," but then claps her gloved hands and wiggles. "This is amazing. Thank you so much."

"No problem. You both have a merry Christmas, okay?" Jack strides quickly back to the warmth of his truck and waves at us as he backs out and continues plows down the street.

I scowl after the truck as I watch it continue to clear the snow off the abandoned country road, but I can feel Gemma's eyes on me. I suppose I'll have to deal with this sooner rather than later. But when I finally look at her, those green eyes are wide with excitement, as if Jack was her own, personal Santa Claus, and the ability to spend Christmas Eve with her family was the only gift she ever wanted.

"We should clean up," I hedge, hoping to have at least a little more time to get my head on straight. Maybe to even talk to her about whatever this was.

"I did already. That's what took me so long." Sure enough, a bag of leftover groceries sits at her feet.

"The fire, though. We have to make sure it's out," I insist.

Gemma shakes her head. "There was a fire blanket next to the fire-place. Plus, it was almost out. I used the blanket and water. We're good."

I study her for a long time, trying and failing to come up with any more reasons to stay. "Well," I finally say. "Let's get you home, I guess."

I'm miserably bad at small talk. Turns out I'm miserably bad at big talk, too. There is a giant elephant in this car with us, and I'm too chicken shit to talk about it. So, we end up making the entire drive back to her parents' house in silence.

But Gemma doesn't say anything, either. She just stares out the passenger window. Even though she's not biting her nails this time, it seems obvious after a while that she's purposely not looking at me. She regrets our time together now that we're in the light of day. I'm sure of it. She's thought this through, realized I'm technically her superior, or that our personalities clash and she'd rather not spend any more time with my grumpy ass than she has to, or that she can't introduce me to her kid. Or maybe even that I'm simply too old for her. Ten years is a lot for some people. Whatever it is, she's over it, and she just doesn't want to break it to me. Back to normal.

I tell myself it's fine. In fact, by the time I've pulled into her parents' driveway, I've decided it's a good call. All of those things are true, and we can't change them just because we had incredible sex. Or just because I think she's adorable and funny. Or that I've never felt this way about a woman before.

A chubby face appears in the window of the house behind an outline of large, colorful Christmas lights that are unlit in the waning daylight. A tree fills the window next to them, and the lights on it twinkle from inside. Nova sees her mom and starts jumping up and down, banging on the glass. A woman who must be Gemma's mother appears behind her and lifts her up gently. They wave at us, and Gemma's entire body leans forward in her seat as if she's being pulled toward them by an invisible force.

But she stays in the car instead of leaping out of it and leaving me in the dust like I expect her to.

"Do you want to come in?" She doesn't take her eyes off her daughter. I'm not sure I heard her right. "What?" I ask.

She turns to me then, her gorgeous eyes almost pleading. "Come in. No one should be alone on Christmas Eve."

I frown at her. "I *like* being alone on Christmas Eve."

She tilts her head and regards me as if she knows I'm full of shit. And maybe I am, but when I glance back at her daughter waiting excitedly for her mom to get out of my car and celebrate the holiday with her, I'm sure I'm making the right decision. Gemma can't just try me out, let Nova get attached, and watch me walk away unscathed. That happened to my own mother one time, and it was enough to turn her off from dating for the rest of her life. I can't allow that to happen to Gemma. She's got a whole life ahead of her. She has other things to worry about besides her own broken heart, if it were to come to that.

No. It's best if I go home, drink my brandy, and cuddle my cat.

I shake my head. "Go spend time with your family, Gemma," I say quietly. "It's what you wanted for Christmas."

She deflates a bit, but perks right up again when Nova leans forward from her grandma's arms to bang on the window one more time. "Okay," Gemma says, resigned. "I'll see you after the holidays, then, I guess."

She shoots me one last questioning glance, as if wondering if maybe I'd want to see each other before then. Of course I do, but I don't even know what that would look like. I'm not going to make promises I can't keep right now, so I nod once.

She blinks rapidly a few times, then swallows before she gets out of the car. I watch her walk all the way to the door, which opens for her as soon as she approaches. Nova practically launches herself into Gemma's arms before she's across the threshold.

It's a sweet reunion, and I know from talking to her on the floor of that dark, cold office that Gemma is over the moon to see her daughter after the impromptu night away. So, I try not to be too hurt that she doesn't even spare me a glance before the door closes behind her.

Chapter 18

Gemma

THE KITCHEN IS AN absolute disaster, as it always is on Christmas Eve. My mom has her famous pot roast in the oven, and vegetable ends litter the countertops. Where there aren't remnants from her cooking dinner, there's flour strewn in white drifts across every other available surface along with trays of about six different kinds of Christmas cookies. Nova won't let go of my neck, so I sit down at the kitchen table with her in my lap, facing me. It allows her to get a better grip with her legs around my middle, but at least my arms get a break.

I grab a recently-frosted sugar cookie off a nearby tray and take a giant bite. "You know Santa only needs one or two cookies, right?" I direct the question over Nova's shoulder to my mother, who is currently squeezing little green trees out of a cookie press.

Mom gives me a long-suffering look. I say something about her cookie-pocalypse every year, and every year, she says the same thing she does now: "Santa's not the only one who needs a little Christmas cheer." Except this time, she follows it up with, "You look like you could use some cheer, yourself."

It only takes one more bite to finish of the cookie. "I mean, I could use a hot shower after sleeping on the floor of a freezing cold house," I grumble around my mouthful.

"Mmm," she hums, unconvinced. "You seem more off than that." She tilts her head as she studies me for a moment. "It wouldn't have anything to do with that handsome man who brought you home, would it?"

I just about choke on the cookie. "What? No." Nova peels her head off my shoulder to look at me. She can't possibly understand the question, but her wide eyes are soaking in the conversation, nonetheless. I cough to dislodge the crumbs from my throat. "No, Mom. I'm tired, that's all. Sleeping on a hardwood floor in front of a fireplace isn't as cozy as it sounds."

"Mmm," Mom hums again. She clearly doesn't believe me, but she's quiet for a minute as she presses two more trees onto the cookie sheet. "You should have invited him in for a bit."

She can't help herself from adding that last bit. She wants me to have a partner because she knows I want that, too. I have ever since I met Nova's father. I really did think he and I would be together forever, but the idea of a baby was too much for him. He left, and I don't know where he went. Haven't heard from him since. Dodged a bullet there, it seems. But even if the bullet didn't hit, it still left a hole.

If only it were as easy as inviting Beckett in. Letting white-walls-and-clean-lines Beckett into this mess would have been a terrible idea. The man can't even handle a teal refrigerator; I'm sure being covered in flour by a toddler at the same time as meeting my parents would have been a disaster. It was for the best that he said no.

Still, my heart hurts a little. "I did," I mumble. Mom's eyebrows shoot up slightly as I clear my throat. "He had things to do."

Mom nods silently, and if she knows I'm lying, she doesn't show it. In fact, she doesn't say anything more about it. She just brushes her hands on her apron and joins me at the table. She reaches out for Nova, who grips me even harder, having sensed she's about to get pulled away.

"Come on, Star-baby. Let Mommy go so she can shower." My mom gently tries to pry Nova from me, but she's got her pudgy little arms wrapped so tightly around my neck that I can barely breathe.

"Why don't you and Grammy get some sprinkles on those cookies so we can bake them for Santa?" I ask, rubbing her back.

"No." The word is high-pitched and staccato, leaving no room for argument.

I squeeze her a bit tighter. "I know. I missed you too, baby. But I stink."

Nova's head pops off my shoulder again. She sniffs a few times, then wrinkles her nose and giggles. "Yucky Mommy."

I boop her nose with my pointer finger, and she laughs again. "Go with Grammy and get the cookies ready, okay? I'll be back in a few minutes."

She reluctantly lets my mom take her. They start singing an off-key and, frankly, unrecognizable Christmas carol, and she's laughing in no time.

Maybe, after a shower, I'll have cleaned Beckett's rosemary scent off of me, and I'll be able to laugh through Christmas Eve, too.

Chapter 19

Beckett

Book, brandy, cat. That's what I want. It's what I do every Christmas Eve.

I repeat it to myself like a mantra as I retrace the route from Gemma's parents' house back to the highway. As if repetition could make it so.

In true suburban fashion, there is a giant mall just before the entrance to the highway. Sitting at the stoplight, I watch as last-minute shoppers crowd the parking lots and wonder if Gemma will be able to sneak away to buy Nova a present.

One of the anchor stores is a bookstore. Seeing it reminds me that I, too, didn't get a chance to get to the store and buy myself a book for the evening. I always buy myself a special new hardcover to crack open on Christmas Eve, but I've been so busy with the Dash house that I hadn't gotten around to selecting one. From the families walking in and out of the store, it looks like they're still open. I might as well stop here since there's no guarantee I'll make it back to my local bookstore before they close for the holiday. Grumbling, I signal and pull into the turn lane.

When I push open the large, oak doors at the entrance, I'm greeted by the warm, vanilla-and-almond smell of new books. I veer straight for the table of new-release hardcovers. With any luck, I'll find something quickly, and then I can be on my way.

But what catches my eye isn't the hardcover books. It's the table next to them that's full of overpriced, impulse-buy toys set out for shoppers to grab for the kids on their way to the checkout.

Gemma was heartbroken about not having a gift for her daughter. There's no way she's going to be able to sneak away to get one this afternoon. The stores close soon, and she won't want to leave Nova, anyway.

Before I can talk myself out of it, I grab the baby doll from the middle of the table and carry it under my arm to the checkout.

It isn't until I'm pulling out of the parking lot and turning left, back toward Gemma's house, that I realize I never bothered to pick out a book.

Chapter 20

Gemma

ONCE I FINALLY MAKE it to the shower, I let the hot water roll over my shoulders until my fingers are prunes. We kept warm enough in the Dash house—even when we weren't engaged in any heated activities—but there's something chilling me down to my bones that I don't think has anything to do with the cold December air. And, sure, I feel pretty shitty about telling Nova I'll be back in a few minutes and then spending at least thirty in the shower, but she's okay. She missed me, but she was fine all night without me.

Being on the other side of it now, I can admit it was actually kind of freeing. I've had two years of being the only parent. Of being the only one who could feed her or calm her or get her to sleep when she was a tiny baby, and then the only one she wanted when she got a little older. I do leave her for work every day, but that feels different. It's a necessity. Leaving her so I can have a little fun on my own? That's revolutionary.

Maybe that's the best I can say for this situation with Beckett—that I learned how to leave my daughter for a little while to take a bit of my life back. And, I guess, if that's all that comes from it, it's not too bad. I hadn't realized how anxious I was about leaving her until last night, but I hadn't realized how badly I needed it until then, either.

Even so, as I look at myself through the steam fogging up the bathroom mirror, I can't help but wonder what it might have been like if we were able to have something more.

Oh well. No sense in dwelling on it, I suppose. We were in it for a fun night. We both made that clear, even if we had danced around the possibility of an extension. What's done is done.

I cross the hallway to the room I share with Nova with a towel wrapped tightly around my torso and another in my hair. I take my time massaging product through my curls in front of the small vanity in the bedroom. As I'm doing that, the doorbell rings. It's probably the same neighborhood carolers who come around every Christmas Eve, and I'm suddenly too tired to stand at the door smiling and pretending they sound good.

Ever-so-slowly, I pull on black leggings, a garish Christmas sweater, and fuzzy Christmas socks. I consider doing my makeup just to be sure the carolers are gone by the time I get down there but decide against it. There's no one to impress here.

I perch myself on the edge of my bed and am just about to scroll aimlessly on my phone for a minute when the unmistakable sound of Nova banging on my parents' piano wafts up to me. The groan that escapes me isn't loud enough to be heard downstairs, but it's close. Why my mother insists on leaving the upright piano open when Nova is around is beyond me. Mom plays sometimes—mostly to entertain her granddaughter—but more often than not, it's Nova herself who puts on a concert for the family. I use the word "concert" loosely; it's more like a cacophony of noise.

When I've persuaded myself that the banging is better than the carolers, I throw open the door to the bedroom. The sound suddenly stops. It's followed almost immediately by a beautiful rendition of "O Holy

Night." It's slightly more upbeat than Beckett's version at the Dash house, but that doesn't help the pang in my heart when those notes float up the stairs.

Jeez, Mom. Twist the knife, why don't you?

Nova lets out a high-pitched giggle, which is imitated almost perfectly by the piano. It makes her laugh even harder.

That's impressive. Mom has really been practicing.

It's the laughter that gives me the push to turn the corner to the living room despite the sadness still tugging at me. Nova always could pull me out of whatever was getting me down. She's magical like that.

But when I get to the living room, I stop in my tracks. Mom isn't playing the piano. She's standing there watching with Dad's arm around her shoulders. I turn slowly to the upright piano against the wall of the living room, and I have to blink a few times before I can process what I'm seeing.

Beckett is sitting on the piano bench, his long fingers flying over the piano keys. Nova is on his lap between his arms, gently pushing random keys as he plays.

It's the sweetest damn thing I've ever seen.

He finishes the song with a flourish. My parents applaud, and Nova also claps her chubby little hands together as she cries, "Again!"

I just stand there like an idiot. I'm not exactly sure what's happening or why he's here, and I'm afraid if I move, he'll disappear up the chimney.

Beckett holds onto Nova as he spins his long legs over the back of the piano bench to face us. His ice-blue eyes meet mine immediately, like he sensed me enter the room a few minutes ago.

"Hi," he says. As if him sitting at my mom's piano in my parents' living room holding my daughter on his lap is the most normal thing in the world.

"Uh, hi?"

"Oh, honey, your coworker here said you forgot this in his car, and he wanted to drop it off for you." Mom holds a bookstore bag out to me. "Isn't that nice?"

I take the bag with numb fingers, my eyes still on Beckett. "I... forgot this?"

"Sure," he says. And if I'm not mistaken, his eyes sparkle with mischief. If I hadn't spent a night with him, I'd think he was the portrait of casual nonchalance, but there's a stiffness to his shoulders that suggests he's wondering if he made the right choice showing up here.

Nova squirms off his lap. He hasn't changed out of his clothes from yesterday, and on top of the wrinkles in them, there's now a streak of flour that Nova leaves behind. I'm sure when he notices it, it'll drive him nuts, but right now, he only has eyes for me.

"Let's go finish those cookies, shall we? Give these two a minute." Mom lifts Nova onto her hip.

"Any chance I can get out of it?" Dad pleads. He's avoided cookie-pocalypse every year since I was a kid. I'm actually surprised he came out of his cave—also known as the den in the basement—to hear Beckett play knowing the cookies weren't finished.

"Nope!" Mom uses her other arm to gently push him toward the kitchen. "I'm down a pair of hands, so yours will have to do." She winks at me as the three of them pass by and out of the room.

Beckett stands slowly but doesn't step away from the piano. "Sorry to ambush you."

"I forgot... what is this?" I ask, lifting up the bag.

"A gift. For Nova," he says gruffly.

I pinch my eyebrows together, confused. "You bought Nova a gift?"

He looks down at the bag in my hand as if it holds the answer. "Well, technically, yes. But you said you hadn't had time to get her anything, so I thought..." he trails off and finally looks up at me. Tears prick at the corner of my eyes. He must see them, because he immediately backtracks. "It's not that I think you can't buy your own gifts. But I figured you wouldn't be able to go out to get her anything, is all. You can pay me back if it means that much to you."

His tone is hard, but is expression is soft. Words are failing me, so I swallow to try to ease the dryness in my mouth as I peek inside the bag. A baby doll stares up at me with big, green eyes.

Nova has an entire play chest full of baby dolls in various states of dress and cleanliness. She found scissors once, so a few of them are also missing chunks of hair. But she won't let us throw any of them away. She pitches an absolute fit any time we try. So we are left with this gruesome play chest full of creepy-ass dolls in the family room. We absolutely do not need another doll. In fact, I had put a moratorium on baby doll purchases after her birthday four months ago.

But my smile stretches wide across my face, almost hurting my cheeks as I meet Beckett's ice-blue gaze. "It's perfect," I say.

He visibly relaxes but stiffens again as if realizing something. "I'll get out of your hair, then. Merry Christmas, Gemma." Beckett says my name gently, like it's a gift he's keeping for himself. He spins on his heel and walks back toward the front door.

It would be devastating to never hear my name on his lips like this again. And that realization propels me forward.

"Sure seems like you don't want to go," I taunt.

He slowly faces me again. "What do you mean?"

"You came all the way back here with a gift for my daughter, lied to my parents about it, then played the piano with a child on your lap wearing wrinkled clothing with a flour stain. Pretty uncharacteristic of you, Becko."

He looks down at himself, then brushes at the flour and smirks. "Don't tell anyone. I have a reputation to uphold."

"Wouldn't dream of it." I tilt my head and narrow my eyes. "Why don't you try something else completely unlike you?"

I fully expect him to scoff and walk out the door, but he takes a step toward me and says, "Like what?"

"Like stay for dinner. Like hang out with us tonight instead of in your sad, lonely penthouse."

"It's not a penthouse," he grumbles, but he takes another step.

"Like spend some time with me when you're not forced to."

"I'm here when I'm not forced to be, aren't I?" Another step. Then another. He's just a few inches from me now.

"Like—"

"Like kiss you under the mistletoe?" His eyes drop to my lips.

"There is no mistletoe," I whisper.

"Funny," he says, circling his arm around my waist and pulling me close. "I could have sworn I saw some. I guess I'll have to try something else, then. Maybe like giving this thing between you and me a shot?"

Beckett brushes his nose back and forth against mine. My breath catches. My heart aches. "You... want that?"

"If you do."

First the gift, then he says he wants to be with me? Call me a snowman in April, because I'm a puddle.

I drop the bag unceremoniously on the floor and wrap my arms around his neck. It only takes a moment for our lips to come together. His hand snakes up my back, and he angles his head to deepen the kiss.

His tongue teases mine, and his rosemary scent overtakes the smell of cookies and pot roast and pine.

I'm about to wrap my legs around his torso and let him pin me against the wall when I hear the paper bag crinkle at my feet. We break apart at the same time and look down to see Nova pull the doll out and squeal.

Beckett chuckles, the sound warm as it vibrates through me. I rest my head on his chest, and he squeezes around my shoulders.

"I couldn't design a better Christmas if I tried," Beckett says into my hair.

"That's because Christmas is supposed to be messy," I tease. He pinches my side, and I jump away from him, giggling.

But he's right. This Christmas is already one of the best I've ever had.

Epilogue

Beckett

One Year Later

"JUST TWO MORE STEPS. That's it. Okay, stop." My hands cover Gemma's eyes as I lead her into the house. Her parents are waiting outside with Nova. This will be her house, too, after all. She deserves to see it tonight, but I want Gemma to see it first.

After we finished the Dash house last January, Gemma wanted to turn right around and buy a tiny, suburban townhouse she'd had her eye on. I convinced her to wait, telling her that she didn't want to jump at the first house she could afford. I also reminded her that she and I flip houses for a living. She could afford a lot more—and actually in the city she loves—if she was willing to flip something.

She grumbled about it for a while, saying that renovating houses was work she wanted to leave at the office. But she eventually admitted I was right and settled on a three-bedroom house in Humboldt Park. It was absolutely trashed when she bought it. Boarded-up windows, garbage everywhere. But the bones were good, and we both saw a lot of potential in it.

That was February. In March, she closed on the house and finally got the keys. She stood in the entryway, hands on her hips and trying not to cough at the smell radiating outward, probably from the kitchen. "This was your idea, Beckles," she said. "You'd better be helping me with this place."

As the months passed, she organized the contractors and paid fees with pride at her ability to do so. I sourced materials for her and gave her some options for finishes and designs. She scoffed at anything white and clean, and I needled her about her more colorful choices.

In short, it was the perfect way to spend time together.

But things sort of fell to the wayside in the summer and into the fall. Nova turned three and started dance lessons, then swim lessons. Gemma spent more and more time at my place under the guise of being closer to the Humboldt Park house, or closer to work... or closer to me. But she didn't seem to be in a hurry to finish the house anymore, which would have been fine by me. I wasn't in a rush for her to have a reason to spend less time at my condo. But I knew what this place meant to her, so I started doing little things while she was busy with Nova. Making sure a faucet was installed here, putting up some wallpaper there.

Eventually, it turned into me taking over the entire design for her. Usually, I hate designing with a homeowner in mind, but being able to do this for Gemma was surprisingly fun. I found myself making choices based on her style and getting excited to show her the things I had selected.

So, when she looked at me with her huge, green eyes and said, "I want to do a reveal like you did for Mrs. Dash!" who was I to argue?

What can I say? The woman has had me wrapped around her little finger since our snowed-in night last year.

When I suggested I reveal the house to her on Christmas Eve, she jumped on top of me and started ripping my clothes off. We made love right there on the sofa in my living room.

I guess it was a good gift idea.

"Can I look yet?" She bounces up and down on her toes, giddy to see her new home.

I take one last look around, needlessly making sure everything is perfect. Of course it is. I've spent every day this month in this place. For her.

"Yes," I say. "Open your eyes."

I watch her as she flutters her eyelids open, then as her jaw drops. She takes in the warm oak finishes and the colorful mosaic tile in the entryway. She gasps when she sees the vintage doorknobs and the ornate stained glass in the panels on either side of the front door.

"Who did you hire to do this?" She eyes me skeptically. "There's no way *you* picked this much color."

I chuckle. "Believe it or not, it was me." My gaze lands on hers. "I did it for you."

The weight of that statement settles on her, and her eyes glisten. "Beckett," she breathes. "It's perfect."

I cup her jaw and press a kiss against her nose, which is still red from the cold. "Come on." I lace my fingers through hers. "I want you to see the kitchen."

She quivers with excitement and allows me to lead her into the space.

She squeals when she sees it. "No fucking way." She doubles over with laughter, releasing my hand to clutch at her sides.

"What?" I ask, feigning innocence. "It's a nice kitchen."

"It's a teal refrigerator!" Gemma forces out between her laughter.

I bite the inside of my cheek to keep my face neutral. "You made such a big deal about the one at the Dash house. I thought you might want one for yourself."

"Bullshit!" Her eyes are watering with glee. "You know I did that to mess with you. I told you that!"

"Did you?" I tap my chin, pretending to think. "I don't remember."

Gemma swats at my arm. I grab her hand before it can hit me and pull her into an embrace. "These things are shockingly expensive," I say. "I'm sure we can sell it and get you a nice stainless steel one."

"You'd like that." She directs her sarcasm into my chest. "Not a chance. It's perfect."

I kiss the top of her head, breathing in her spice-and-sugar scent. "*You're* perfect."

She tilts her face up to me, her green eyes sparkling and her lips pursing against a smile. "Even though I'm keeping the teal fridge?"

I lean in for a kiss. "Especially because you're keeping the teal fridge. I love you, Gemma Woodard. I wouldn't have you any other way."

"I love you, too, Beckett Camdon." She kisses me back. "Thank you for putting away the white paint for me."

I'd do that for her and then some, which she must know as she tours the rest of her dream home and sees the color on the walls, the vintage finishes, and the Christmas decorations from her childhood that her mom came over and helped me place.

And later that night, after her parents have gone home and we've tucked Nova into her new bed, we spend our first night of many in Gemma's new bedroom, designing our future.

Acknowledgements

I'VE SAID IT BEFORE, and I'll say it again. I am beyond lucky to have such an incredible team in my corner. This book wouldn't be what it is without them.

First and foremost, a huge thank you to my husband. These books simply don't exist without him. Thank you for watching Christmas romcoms with me, sitting up on the couch late at night to keep me company while I work, and taking the kids when I need some space. You're my favorite, and I love you.

A massive giant thank you to my early readers. Your feedback and cheerleading has been invaluable. Thank you to: Hannah, Jillian, Alexis, Stefanie, Caitlin, and Jessica. Your comments gave me life on this one, and I'm so glad to have you all in my corner.

Thanks also to my street team! April, Ashley, Catarina, Courtney, Hana, Hope, Jen & Victoria, Kae, Kathy, Kayla, Laura, Leah, Lexi, Lindsey, MC, Mindy, Sarah, Sarah, Sarah (that's not a mistake!), Savannah, and Trish & Ash. Thank you for helping me spread the word and cheering me on.

A big thank you to my agent, Katie Monson at SBR Media. Thanks for helping me bring my stories to new readers and believing in me.

And of course, this amazing cover. Jillian Liota of Blue Moon Creative Studio took my bare-bones ideas for this one and really ran with them. It's so cute, and so perfect. Thank you.

My dear, dear friend, Megan Carver... how do I even begin? Thank you for being a sounding board for ideas on this one—Emelia Dash is for you.

Thank you to my family and friends. Your support means everything. Thanks, especially, to my mom, dad, and brother who were tortured with my very first stories when I was a kid. I think, I've come a long way. Hopefully this one's not too spicy. And thank you to my sister-in-law who has been endlessly supportive. I still have that Christmas wrapping paper, and I'm excited to hang my ornament this year.

Last, but not least, thank you to my readers. These books are for you. Thank you for loving them.

Also By Allie Samberts

Leade Park:
The Write Place
The Write Time
The Write Choice

Standalones:
Common Grounds

A new childhood friends to lovers, sunshine/sunshine, dual point of view romance coming Spring 2025!

Stay up to date on new releases and grab some bonus content! Subscribe to Allie's newsletter at https://alliesamberts.substack.com

About the Author

Allie Samberts is a romance writer, book lover, and high school English teacher. She was voted funniest teacher of the year for 2023 by her students, which is probably her highest honor to date. She is also a runner, and enjoys knitting and sewing. She lives in the Chicago suburbs with her husband, two kids, and a very loud beagle. You can follow her on Instagram @alliesambertswrites, read her blog at alliesamberts.substack.com, and get other updates at www.alliesamberts.com.

Made in United States
Troutdale, OR
12/14/2024

26413306R00083